Really really stupid.

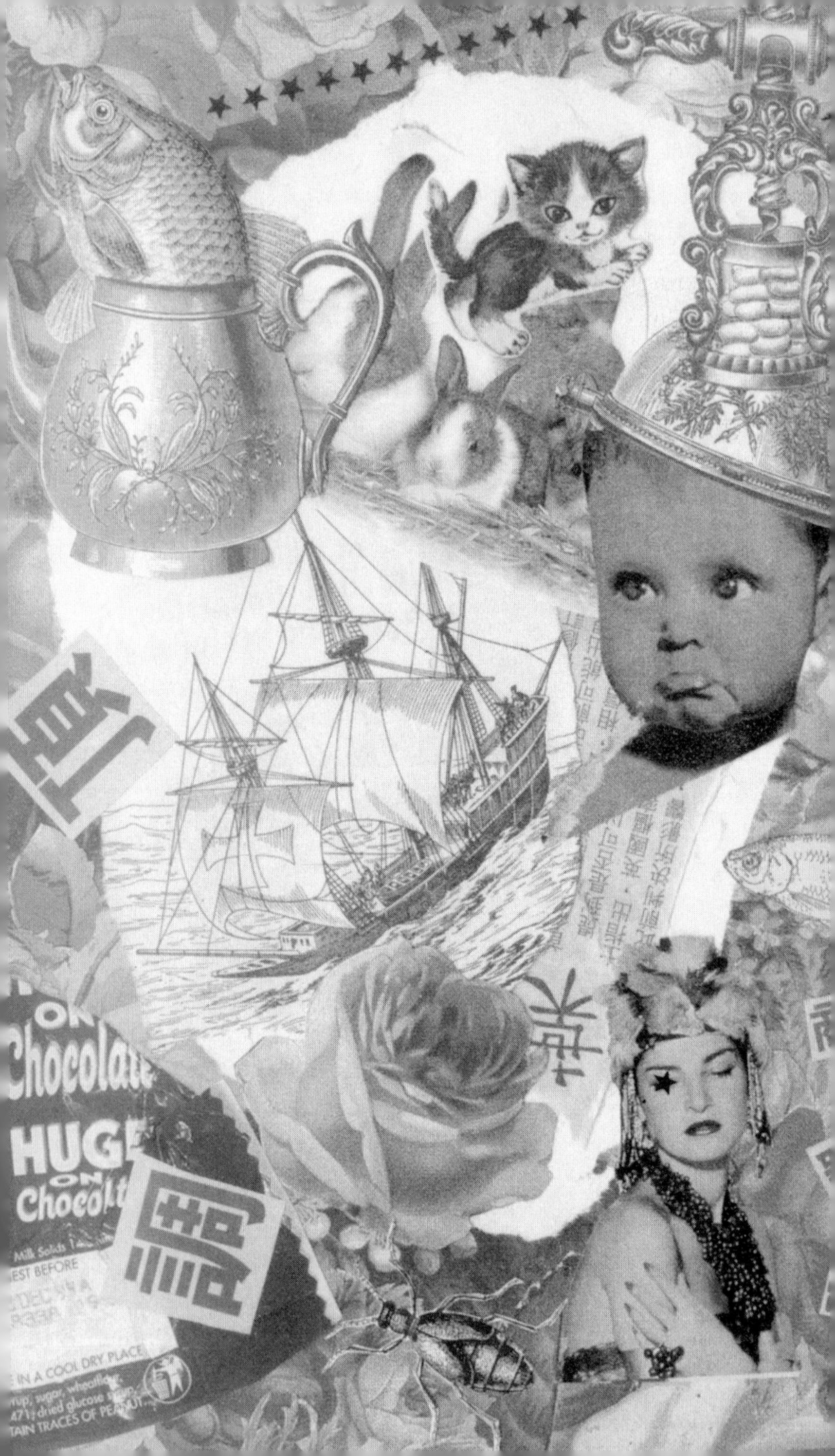
Chocolate
HUG
ON
Chocol
Milk Solids
BEST BEFORE
IN A COOL DRY PLACE
TAIN TRACES OF PEANUT

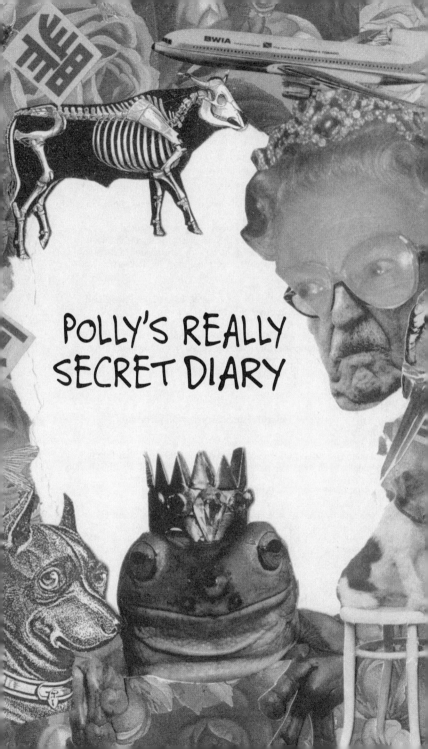

POLLY'S REALLY SECRET DIARY

Published by
Delacorte Press, an imprint of
Random House Children's Books
a division of Random House, Inc.
1540 Broadway
New York, New York 10036

First American edition 2002
First published in Great Britain by Bloomsbury Children's Books in 2000

Visit us on the Web! www.randomhouse.com/kids
Educators and librarians, for a variety of teaching tools, visit us at
www.randomhouse.com/teachers

Library of Congress Cataloging-in-Publication Data

Thomas, Frances.
    Polly's really secret diary/Frances Thomas; illustrated by
Sally Gardner.
    p. cm.
    Summary: In her illustrated diary, Polly writes about her family,
her plans to run away, her school friends and ex-friends, and her boring
hamster Horace.
    ISBN 0-385-72902-2—ISBN 0-385-90049-X (GLB)
    [1. Family life—England—Fiction. 2. Schools—Fiction.
3. Friendship—Fiction. 4. England—Fiction. 5. Diaries—Fiction.]
I. Gardner, Sally, ill. II. Title.

PZ7.T36665 Po 2002
[Fic]—dc21

The text of this book is set in 13-point Times New Roman Schoolbook.

Manufactured in the United States of America

June 2002

10 9 8 7 6 5 4 3 2 1

BVG

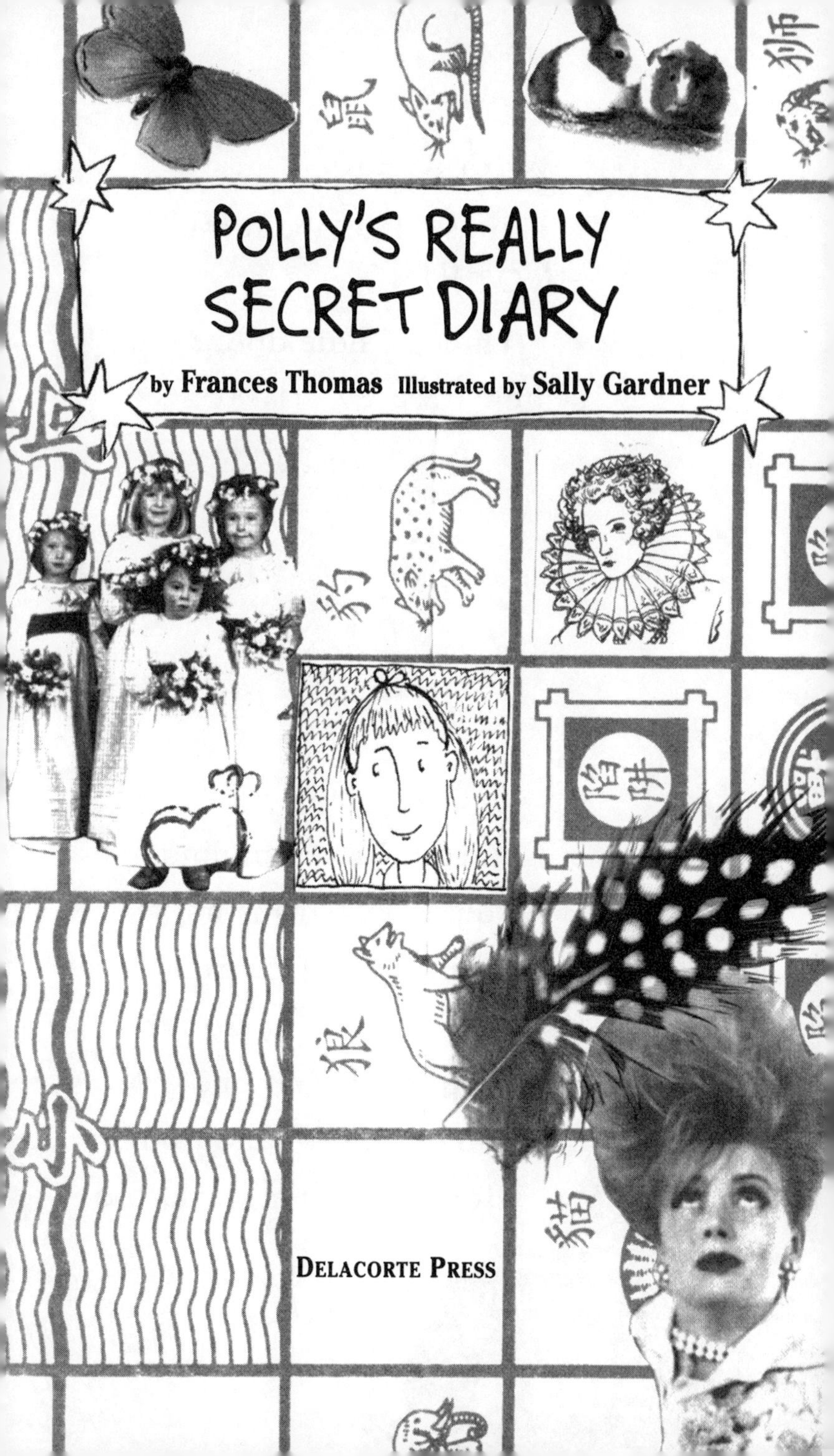

POLLY'S REALLY SECRET DIARY

by **Frances Thomas** Illustrated by **Sally Gardner**

DELACORTE PRESS

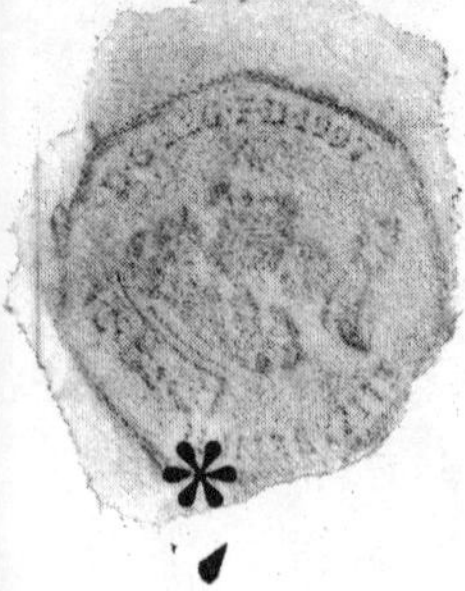

Wednesday

Things I like about my life: NOTHING.

Things I hate about my life: EVERYTHING.

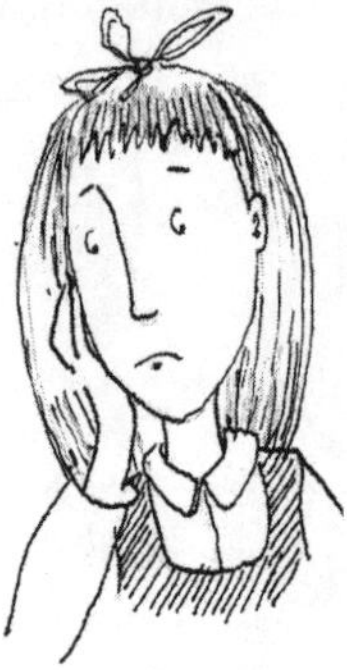

Thursday

Anyway, I am Running Away soon. This is my Running Away Diary.

I am saving up. So far I have got 75p and one Double Decker candy bar.

Horace has run away too.

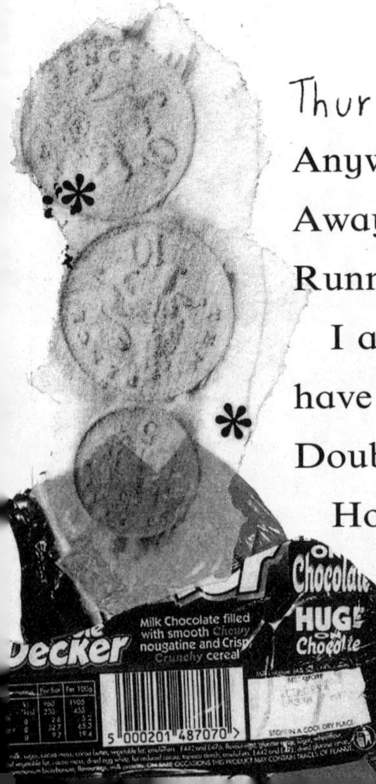
Decker
Milk Chocolate filled with smooth Chewy nougatine and Crispy Crunchy cereal
Chocolate
HUGE
Chocolate

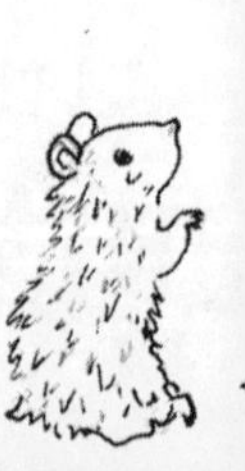

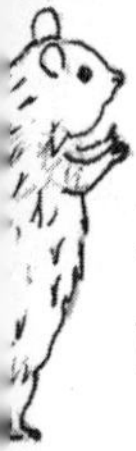

- away

He is our hamster. He has been missing two days.

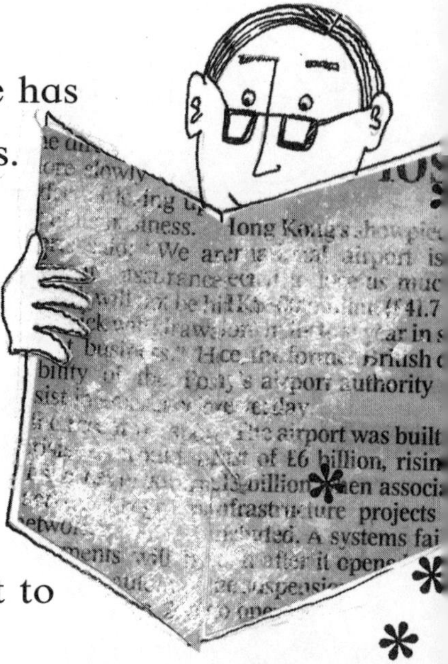
airport was built

Dad says he will come back but how does he know?

They pretend they know everything but they don't.

They say things just to shut you up but I am NOT SILLY.

I said to Mum, it is not fair, Kelly isn't my best friend anymore. Yesterday she was my best friend but today she said Lisa was going to be her best friend and anyway she had a secret. I said that it was not

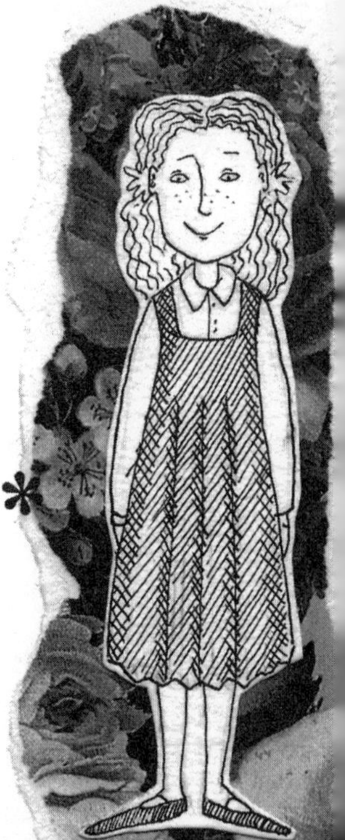

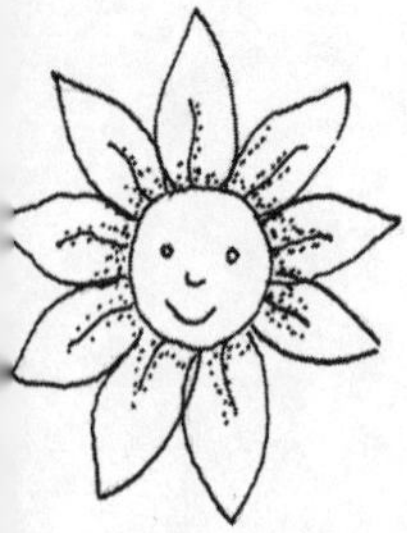

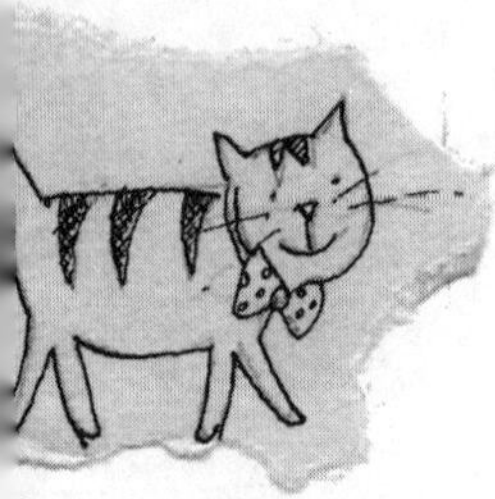

fair of people to be your best friend one day and then change their minds. It is silly of her to keep having secrets. All Mum said was, not now darling. She should listen to me when I am telling her things.

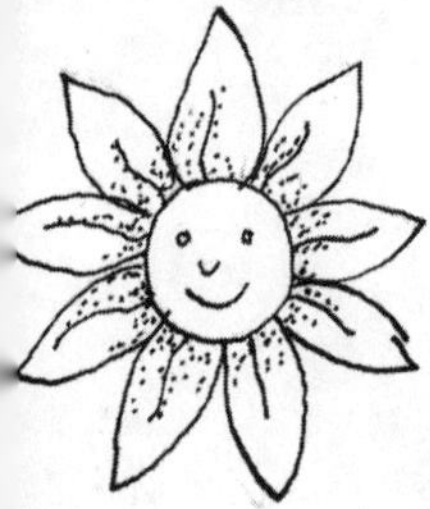

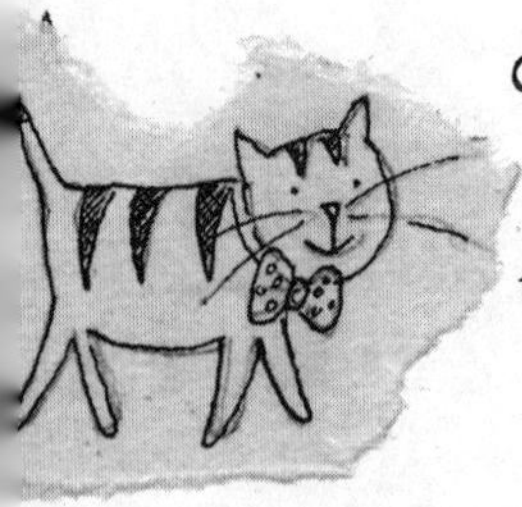

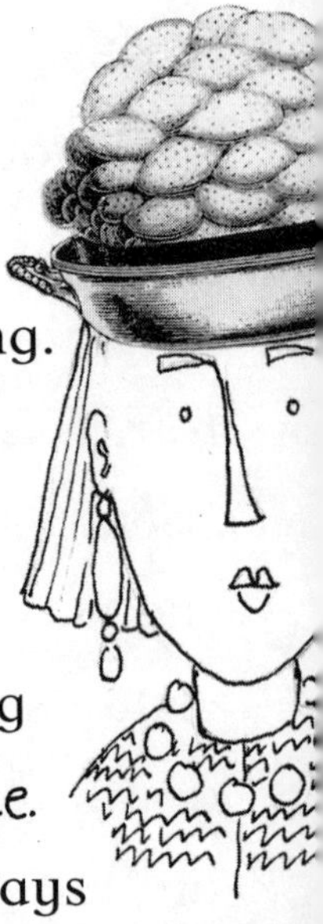

Friday

Miss Price says you can't just hate something. You have to say why.

I hate her. She is a der-brain.

Mum says I am going through a Stroppy Faze.

I hate her. She is always

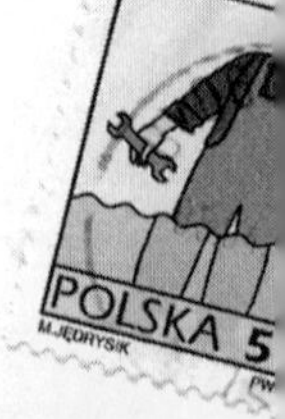
POLSKA

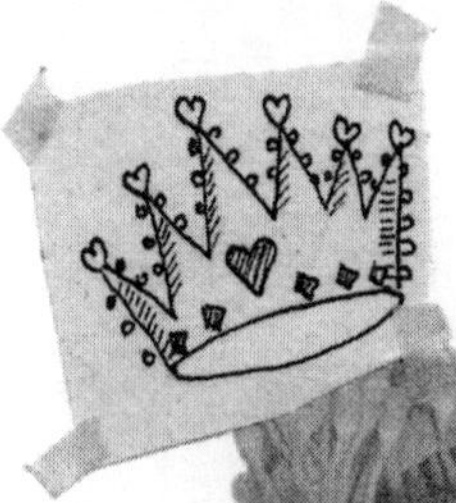

going on at me to:

Tidy Your Clothes
Don't Shout at Mopsy
Wear Skirts
Eat Your Brocerly.

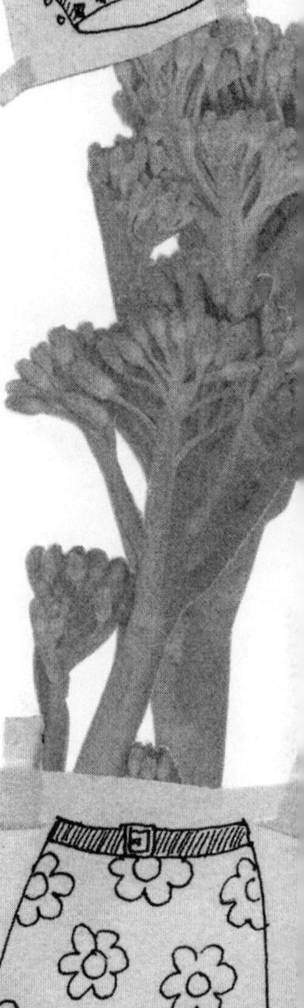

Dad says, what happened to my dear little Princess?

He is IRRITATING me.

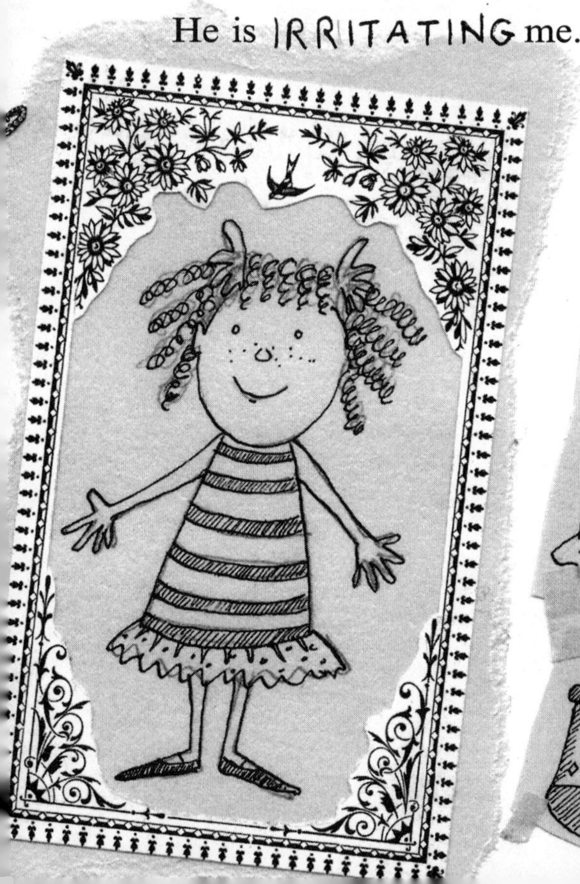

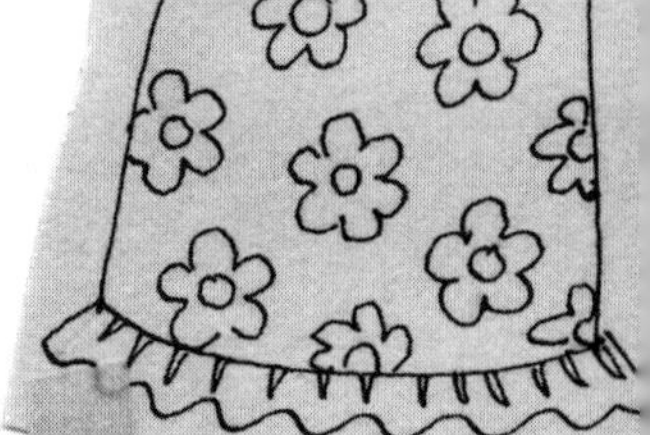

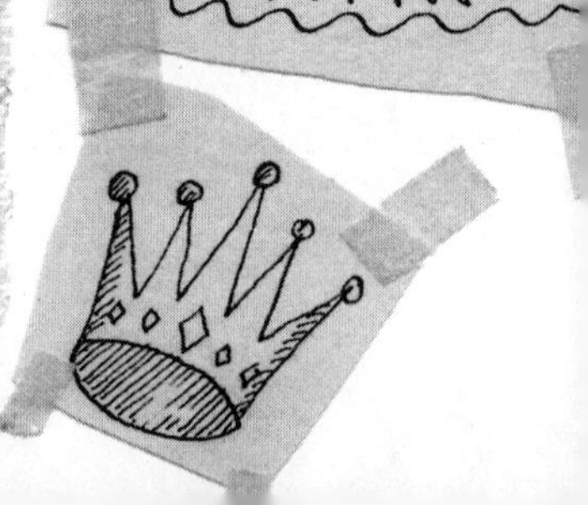

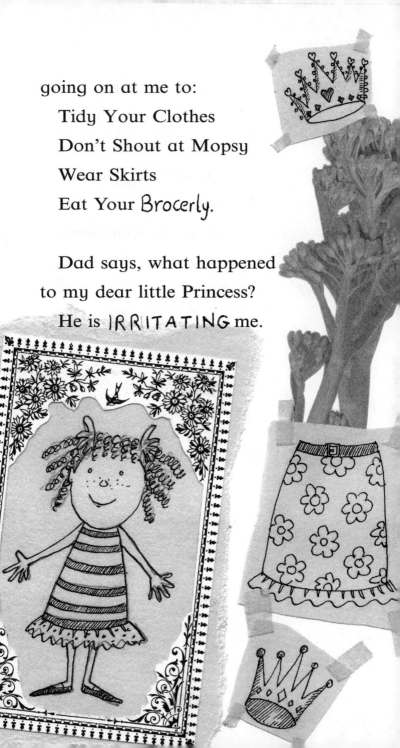

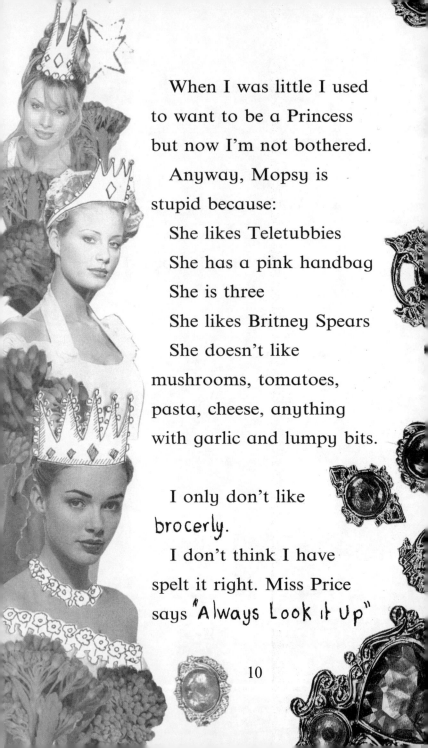

When I was little I used to want to be a Princess but now I'm not bothered.

Anyway, Mopsy is stupid because:

She likes Teletubbies

She has a pink handbag

She is three

She likes Britney Spears

She doesn't like mushrooms, tomatoes, pasta, cheese, anything with garlic and lumpy bits.

I only don't like brocerly.

I don't think I have spelt it right. Miss Price says "Always Look it Up"

10

but why should I look it up when I don't even like it?

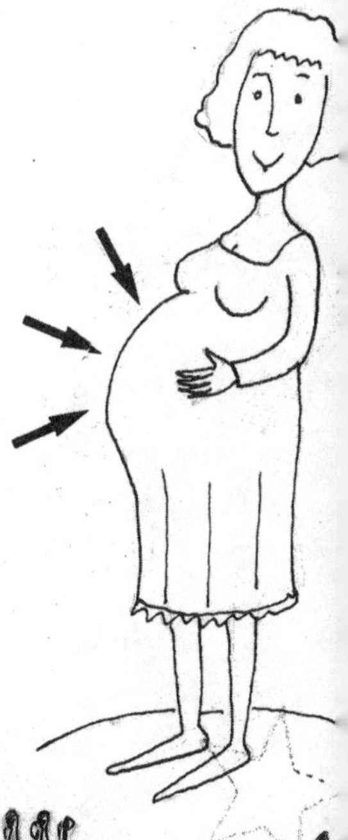

Mum is always tired. She says it will be better when the new baby comes.

WHO WANTS A NEW BABY ANYWAY— NOT ME!!!

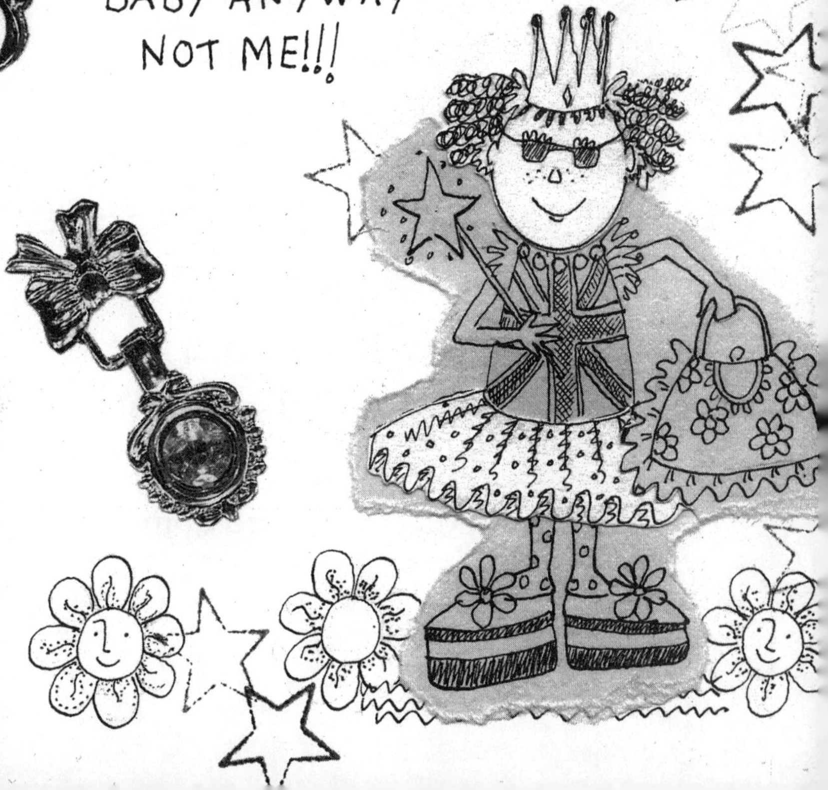

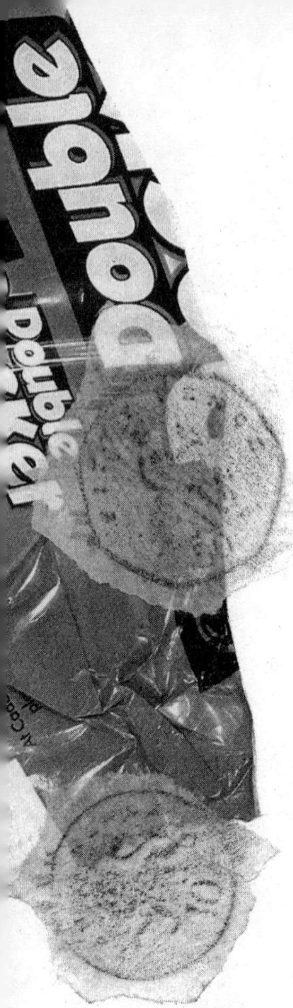

I think it is unfair of her to say the **new** baby all the time. She should think about her proper children a bit more.

Horace has been away three days.

I still have 75p.

I have one Double Decker and a sandwich from tea.

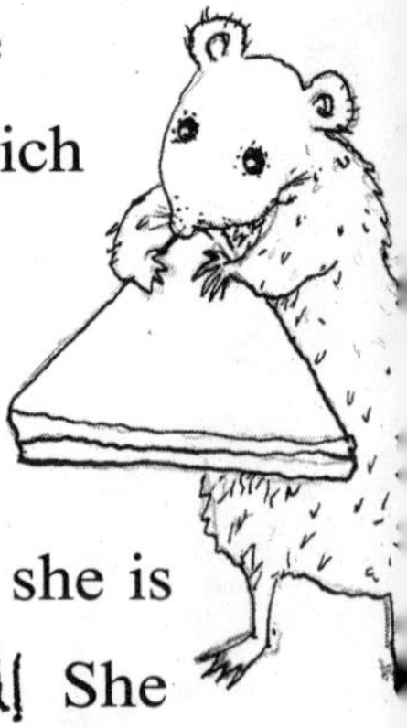

Monday

Kelly's secret is that she is going to **Disneyland!** She is going on and on about it. They are going in the holidays. They are going

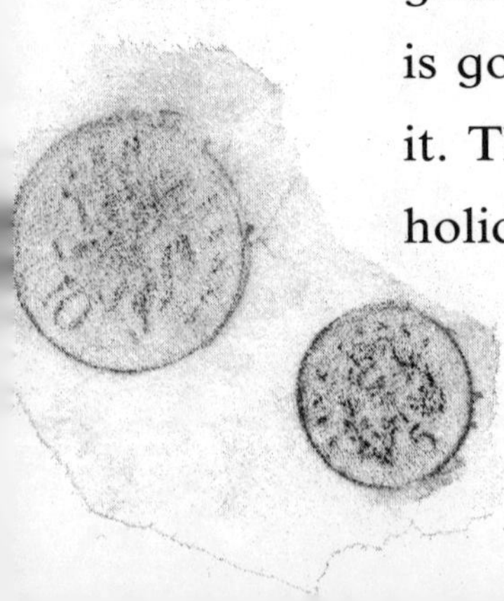

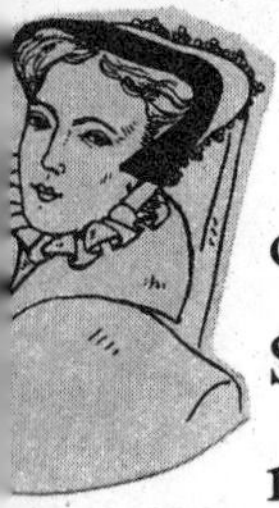

on the train to France. She says she won't bring me a present. She will bring Lisa a present.

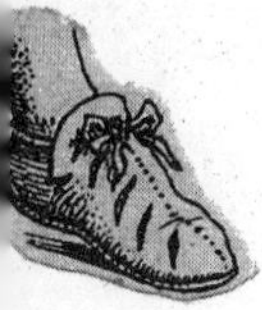

I don't care. Disneyland is smelly.

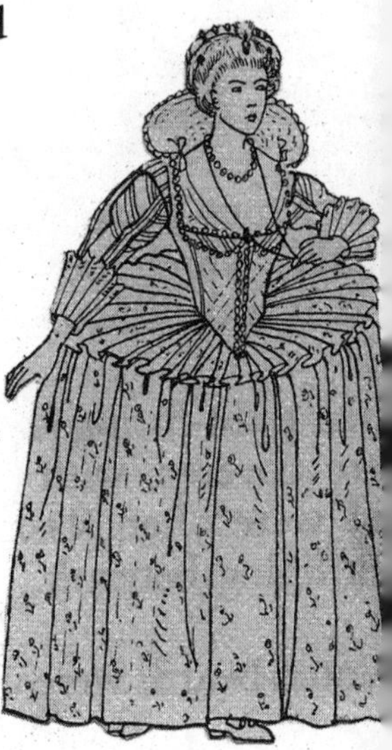

Kelly isn't my best friend. She used to be my best friend.

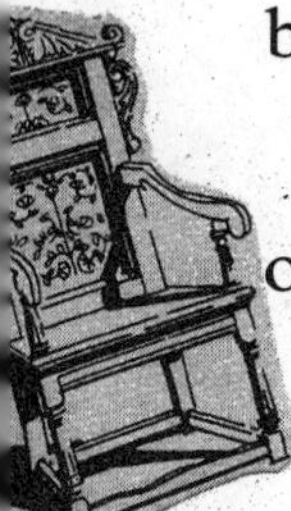

Some people always go on and on about things.

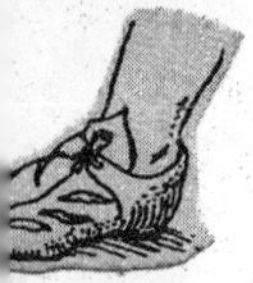

We are starting the Tudors. They lived in wooden houses and threw their poo out of the windows. I said, I think the Tudors were smelly. Miss Price said they

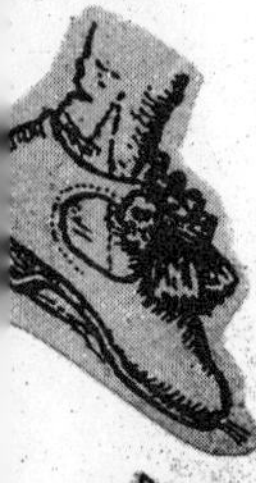

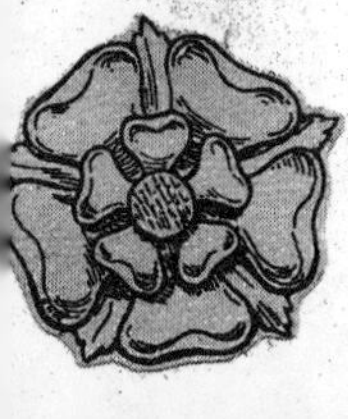

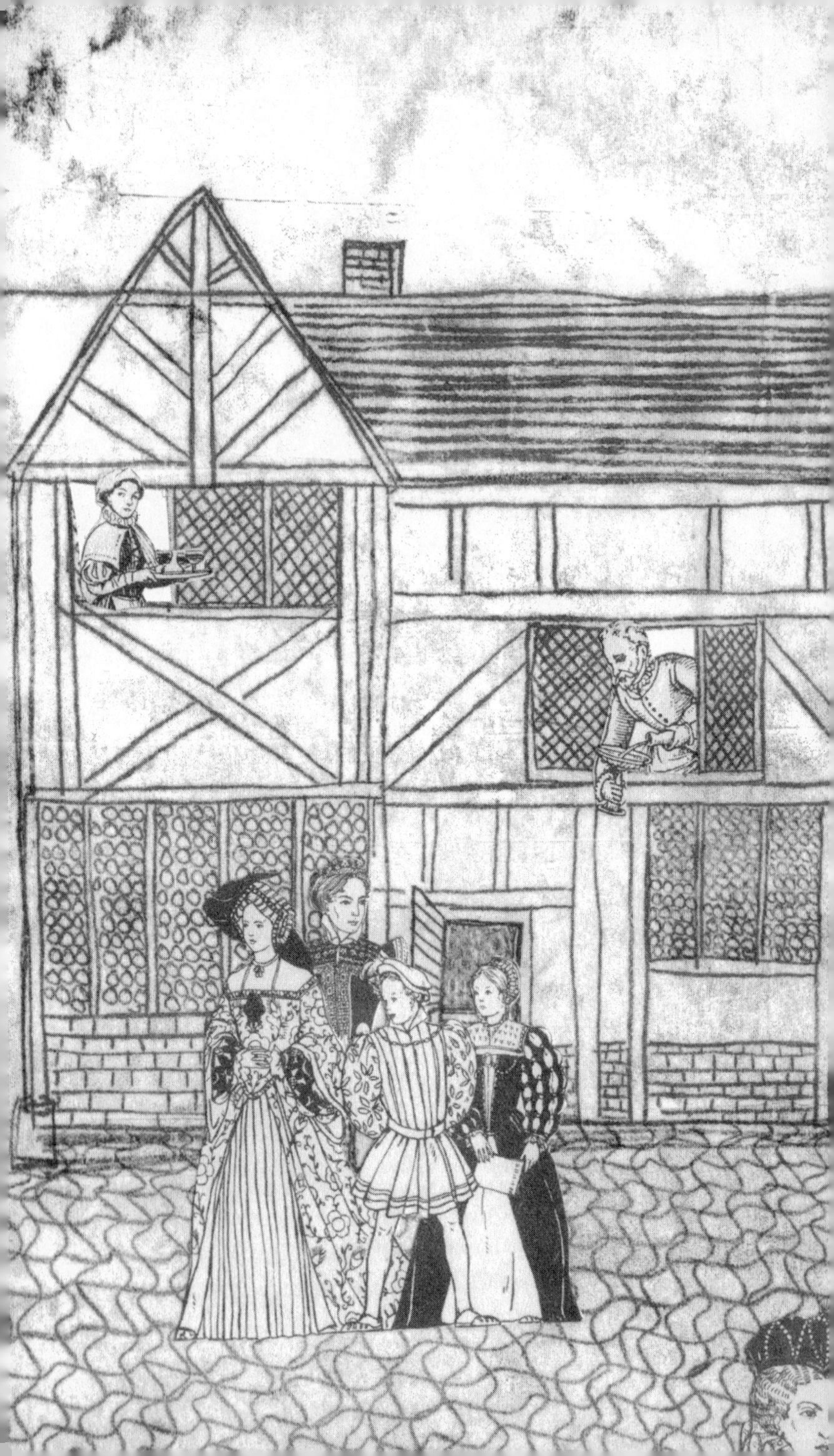

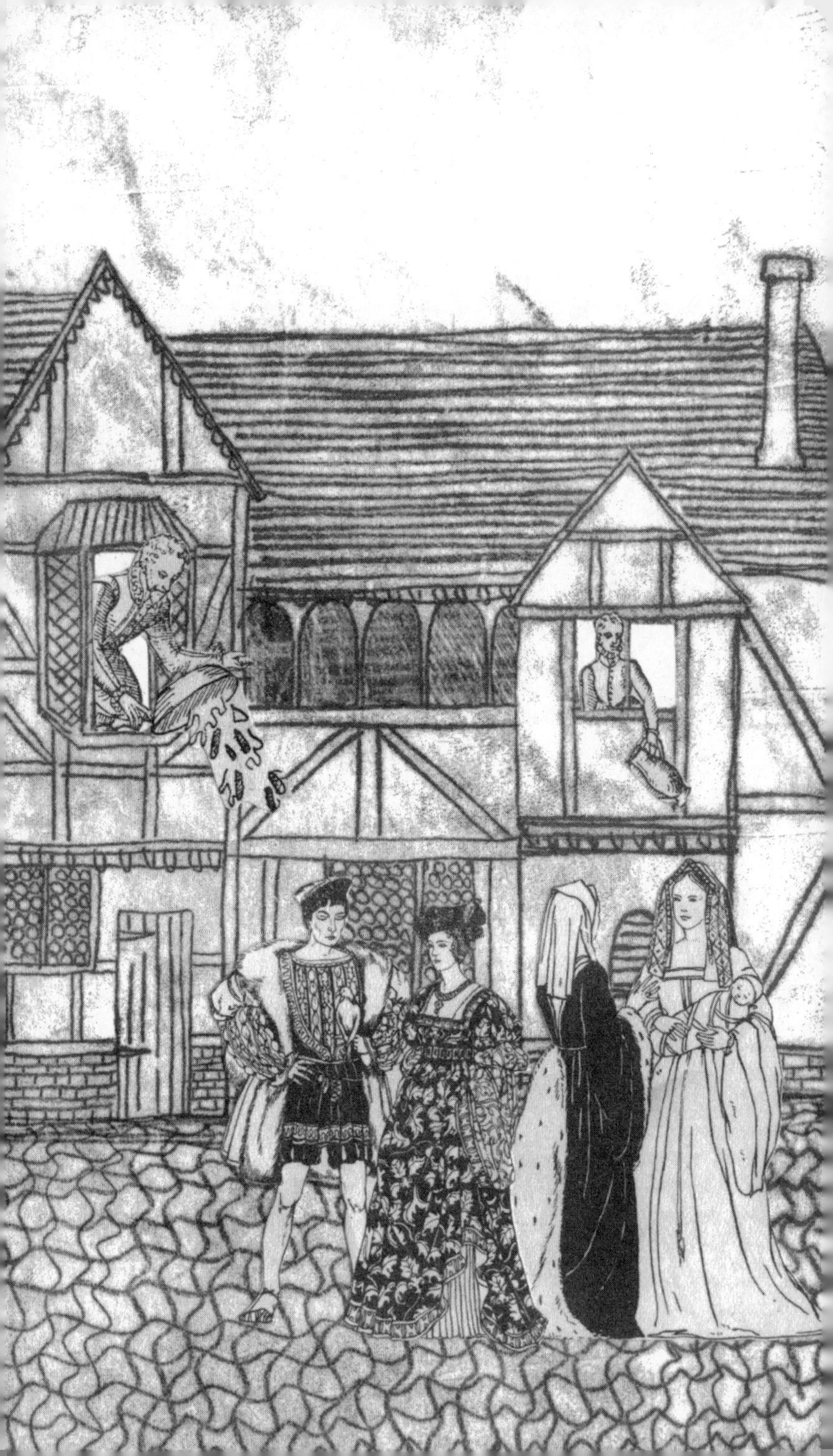

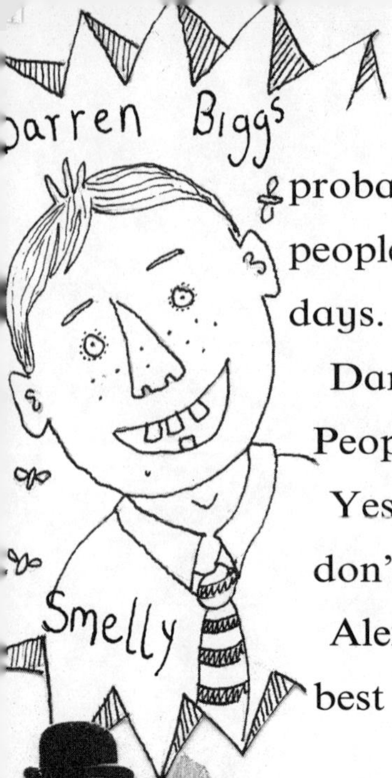
Darren Biggs
Smelly

probably were, but then people were smelly in olden days.

Darren Biggs said Some People are still smelly.

Yes, like Darren Biggs. I don't like him anyway.

Alex will probably be my best friend now.

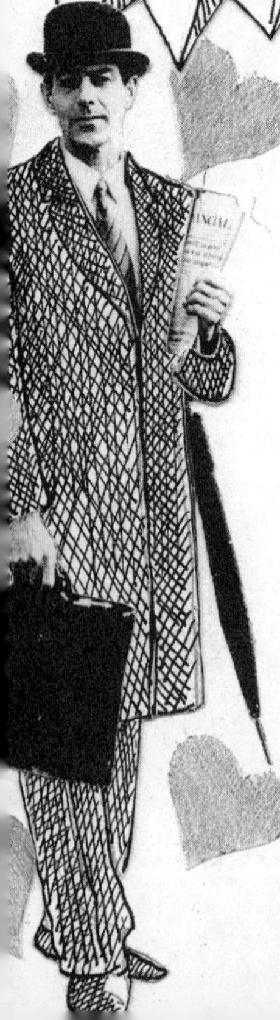

Miss Price is called Julia. She is twenty-seven. Her boyfriend is Nigel. He is In Banking.

She is not getting married yet but she might next year. She will get married in a Registrar Office. She doesn't want bridesmaids.

She should not wear Pink. It matches her nose. She should wear blue or green. And not dangly earrings.

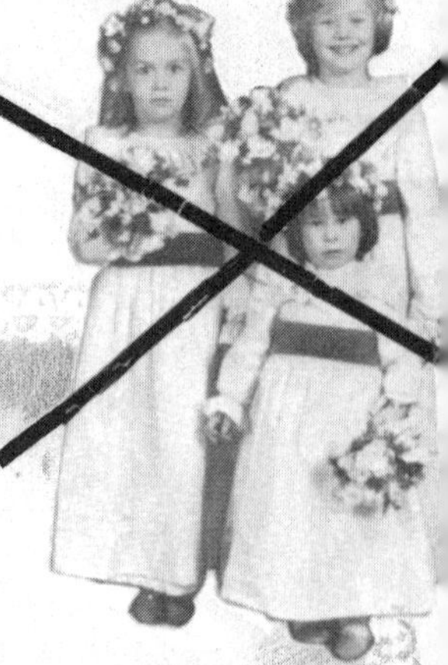

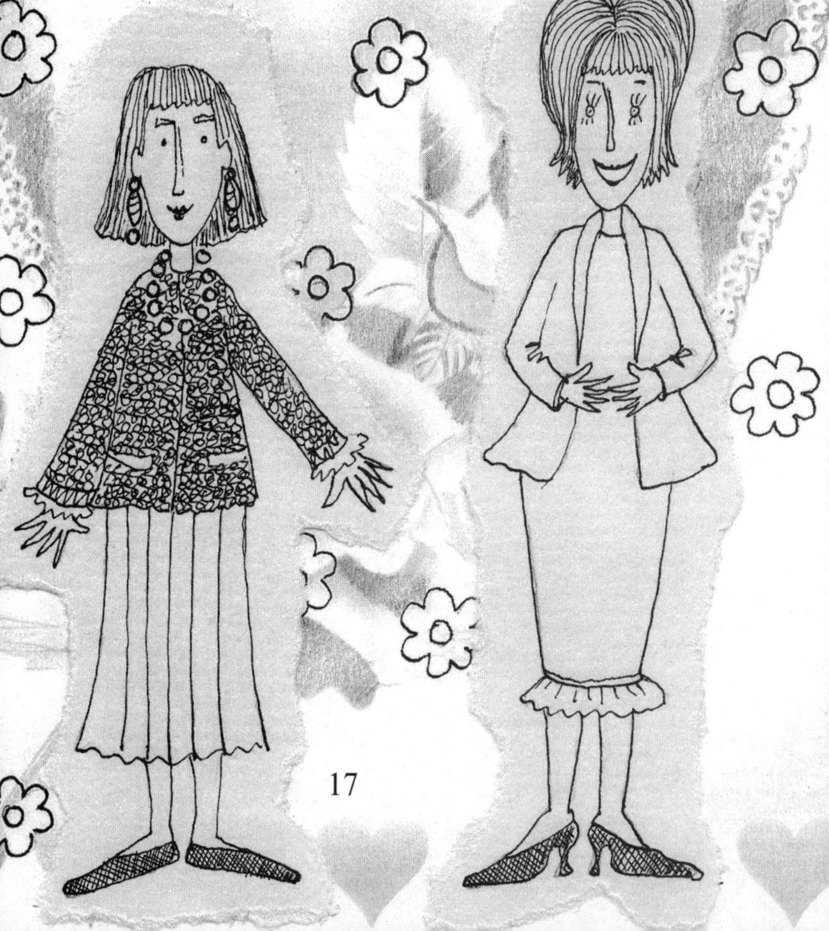

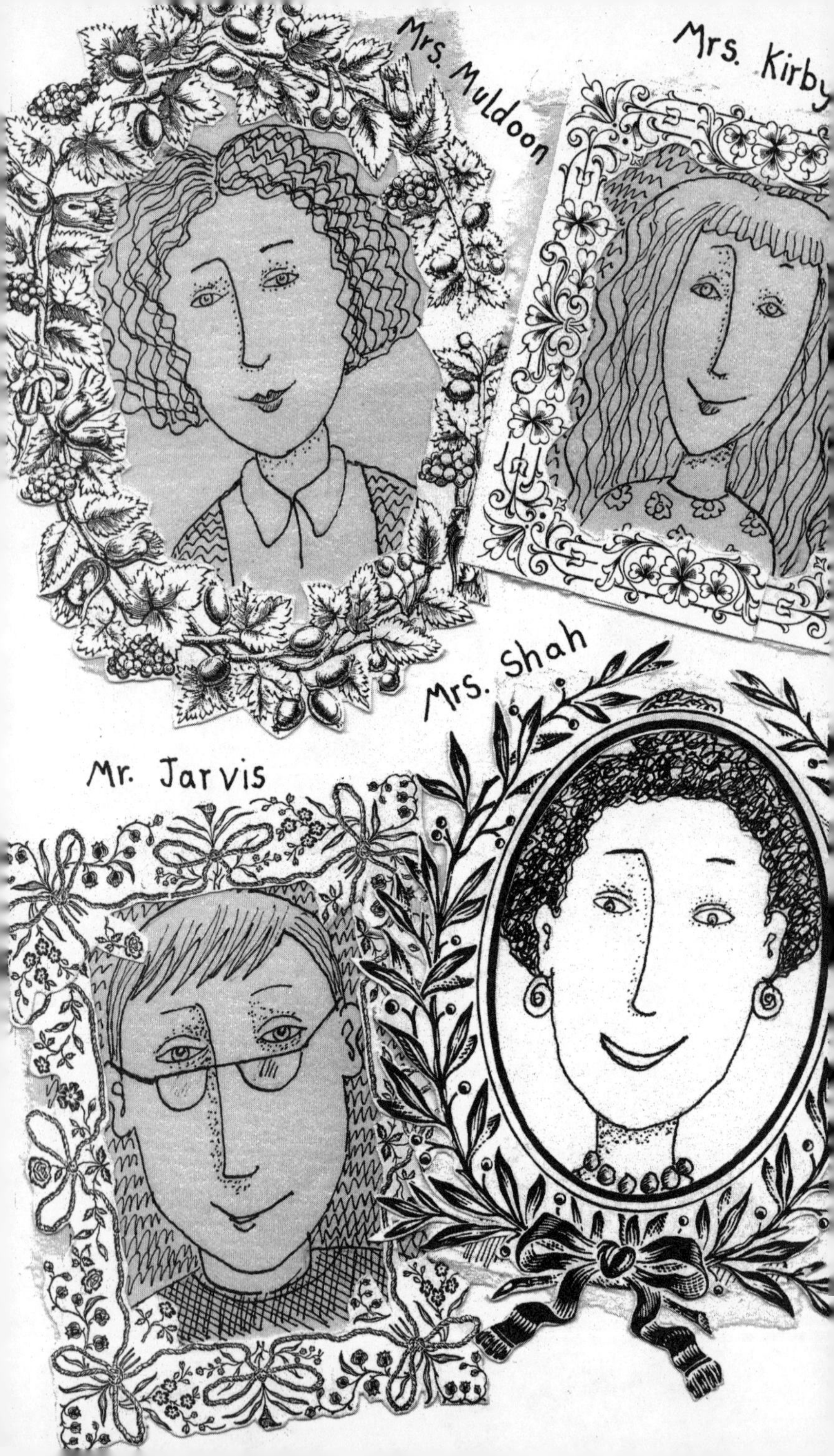
Mrs. Muldoon
Mrs. Kirby
Mrs. Shah
Mr. Jarvis

Mrs. Muldoon is our Headmistress. She is nice sometimes, except when she is being nasty.

Last year we were in Mrs. Kirby's class. She was brilliant. Next year it will probably be Mr. Jarvis or Mrs. Shah. I hope Mrs. Shah.

It's not fair. I said to Dad, can we go to Disneyland because Kelly's going to Disneyland and he said, ooh Polly. He said, I don't think so pet, not this year anyway because of the new baby and not having lots of money.

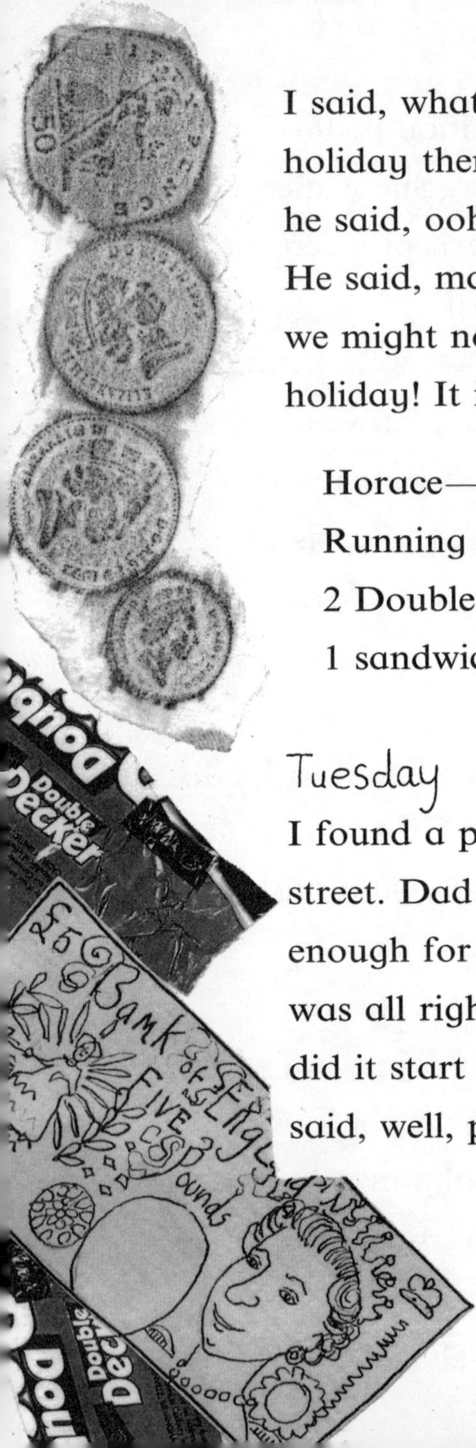
Double Decker
FIVE
Pounds

I said, what will be our holiday then this year, and he said, ooh Polly again. He said, maybe this year we might not have a holiday! It is so not fair.

Horace—6 days
Running Away Money—75p
2 Double Deckers
1 sandwich

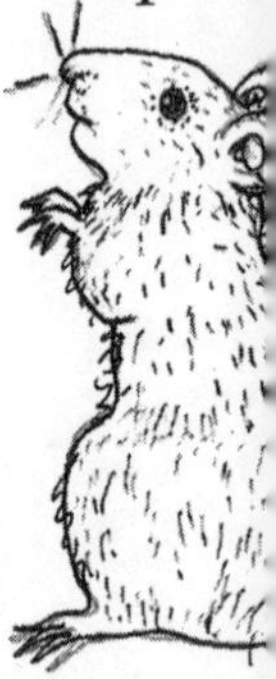

Tuesday

I found a penny in the street. Dad said it wasn't enough for stealing, so it was all right. I said, when did it start being stealing? He said, well, perhaps £5.

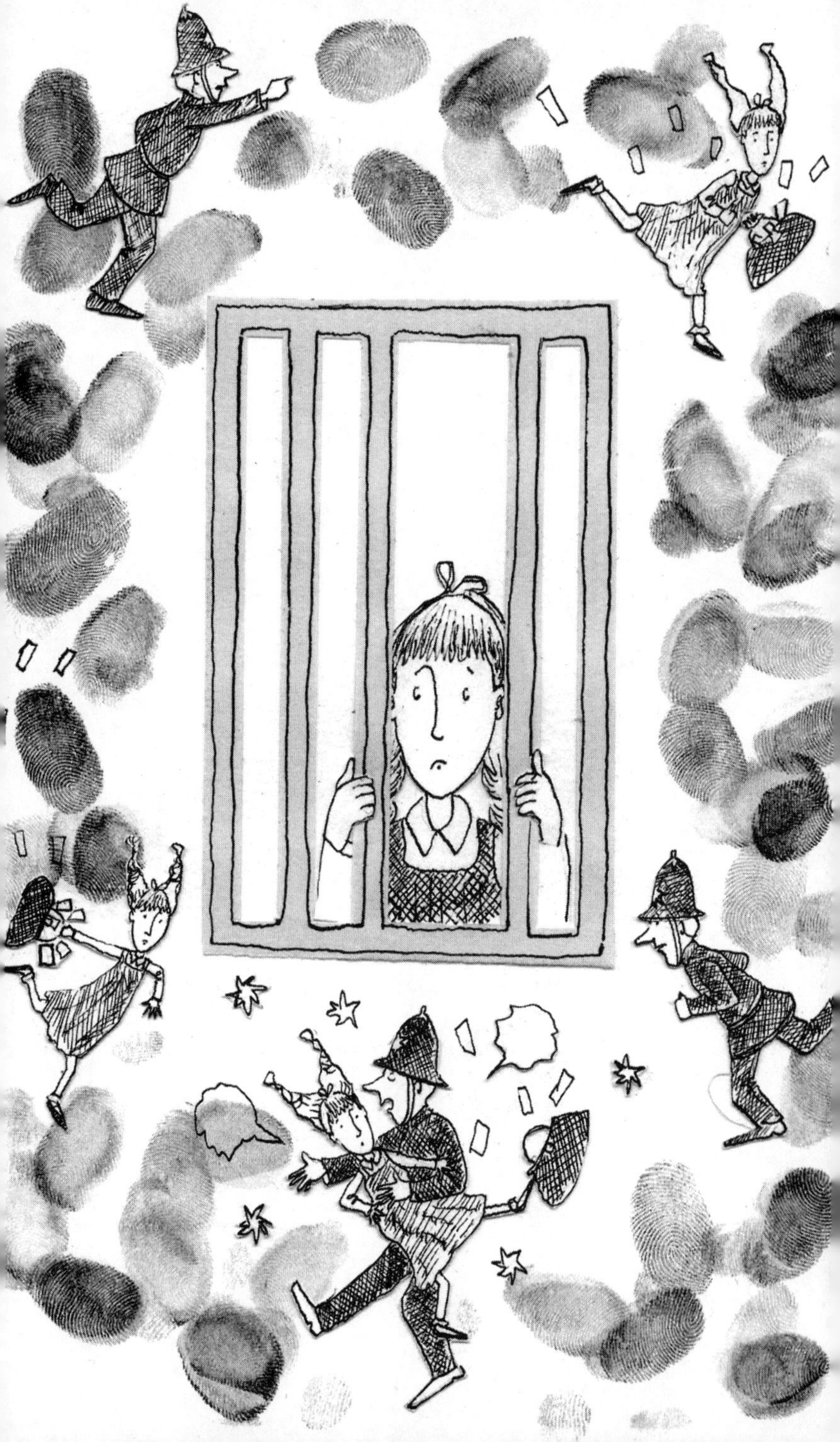

I said would 10p be? He didn't know.

I said would 5p be? He said, oh Poll, stop asking questions.

In school we talked about holidays. Kelly went on and on about Guess What. Luke is going to Italy and Trixie is going to Spain. Oliver said they went to Italy last year and he said they had

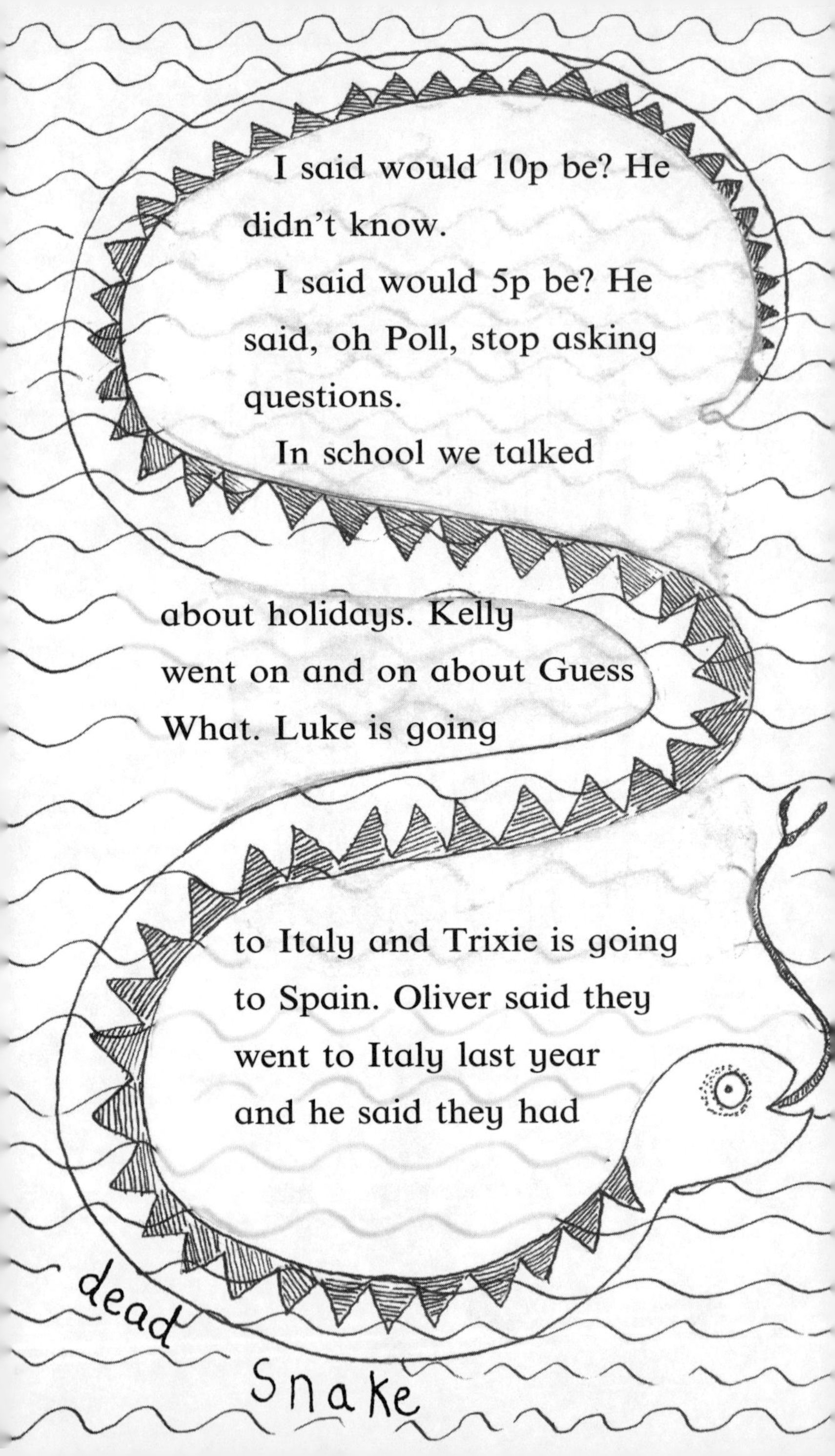
dead
Snake

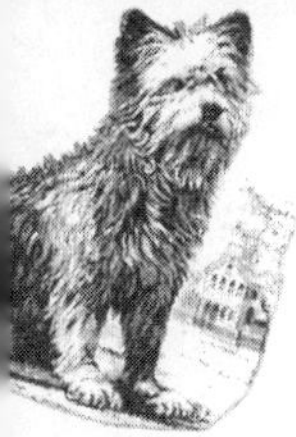
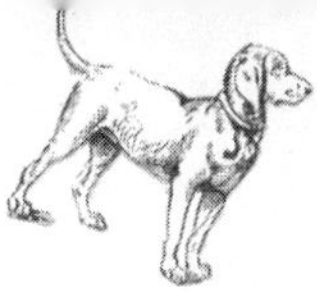
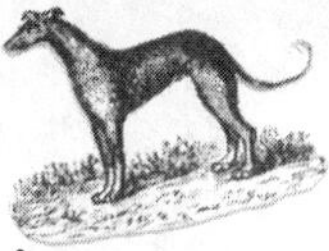
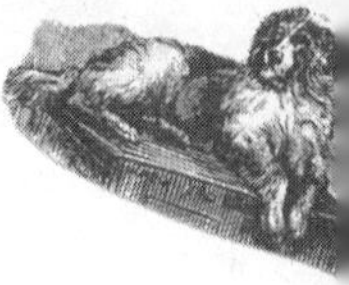

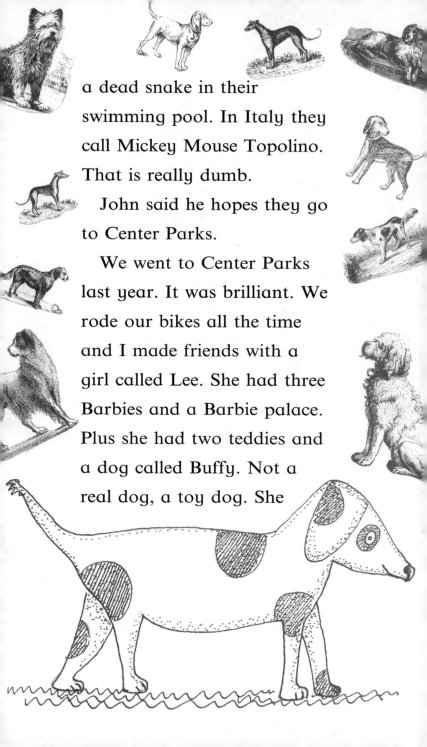

a dead snake in their swimming pool. In Italy they call Mickey Mouse Topolino. That is really dumb.

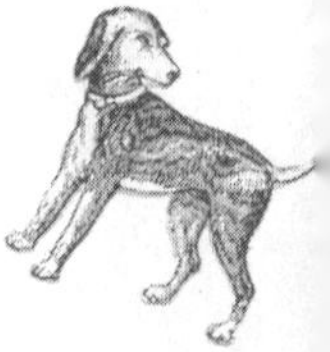
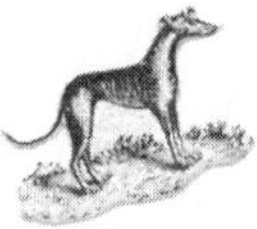

John said he hopes they go to Center Parks.

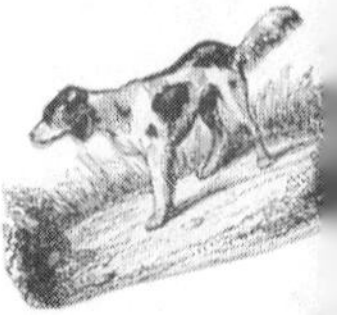
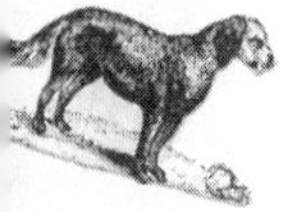

We went to Center Parks last year. It was brilliant. We rode our bikes all the time and I made friends with a girl called Lee. She had three Barbies and a Barbie palace. Plus she had two teddies and a dog called Buffy. Not a real dog, a toy dog. She

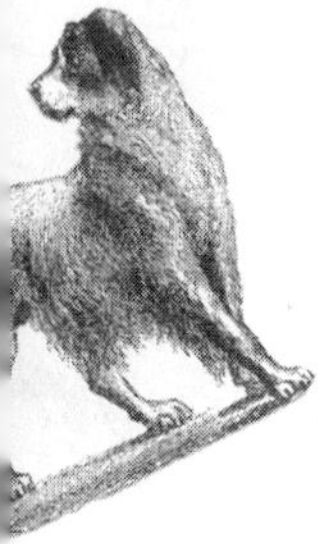
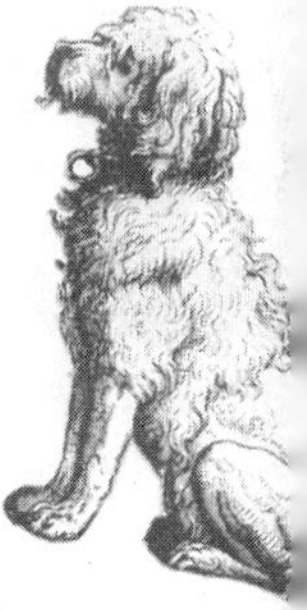
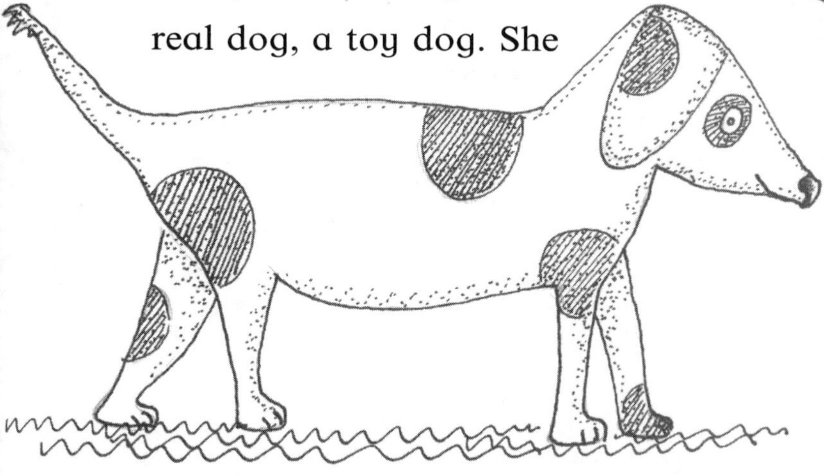

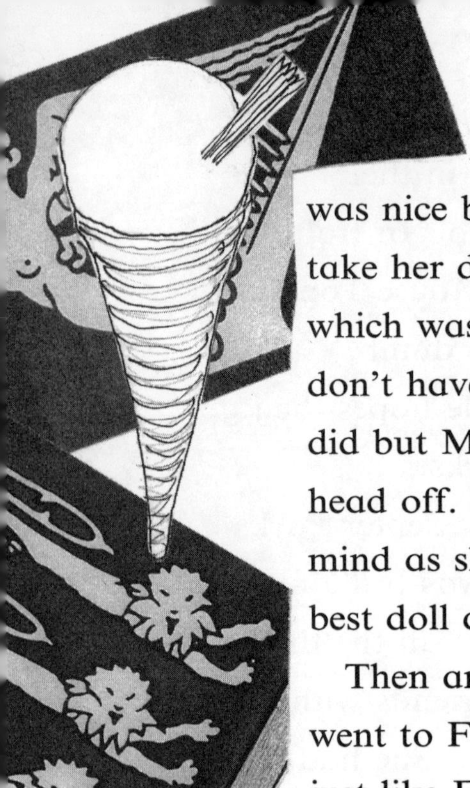

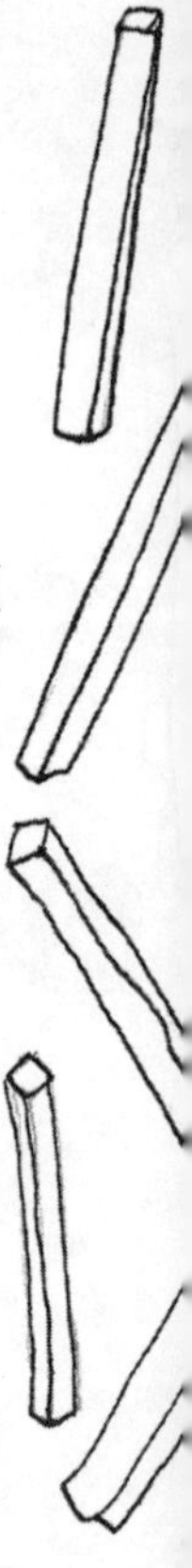

was nice but she had to take her dolls everywhere, which was a bit boring. I don't have a Barbie doll. I did but Mopsy pulled the head off. I don't really mind as she wasn't my best doll anyway.

Then another time we went to France. France is just like England except the people speak very fast in French all the time. You say glas For ice cream and pomfreet for French fries. Mercy bocoo—I don't know how you spell it—is thank you very much. You have to be

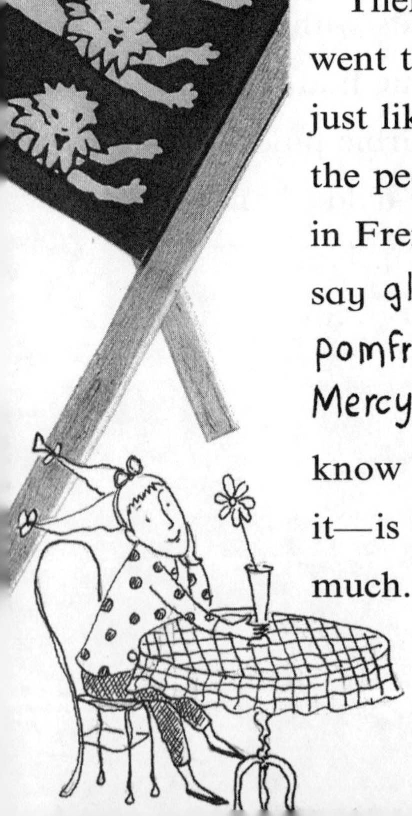

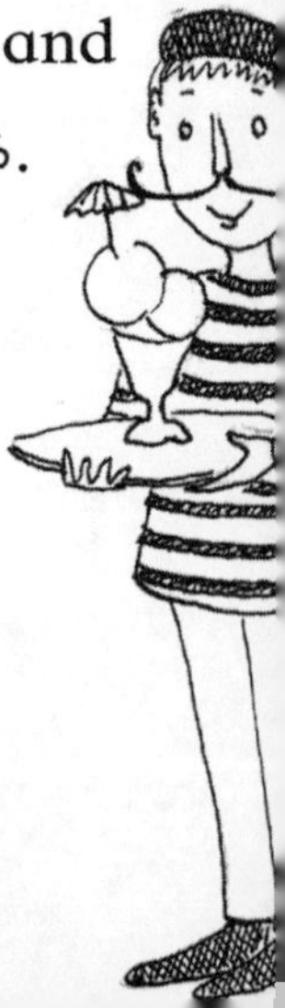

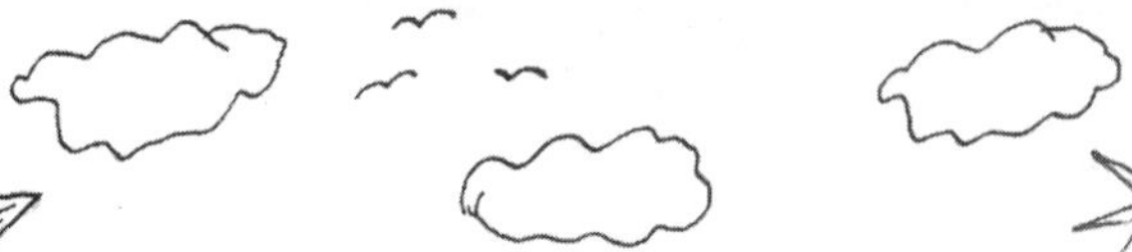
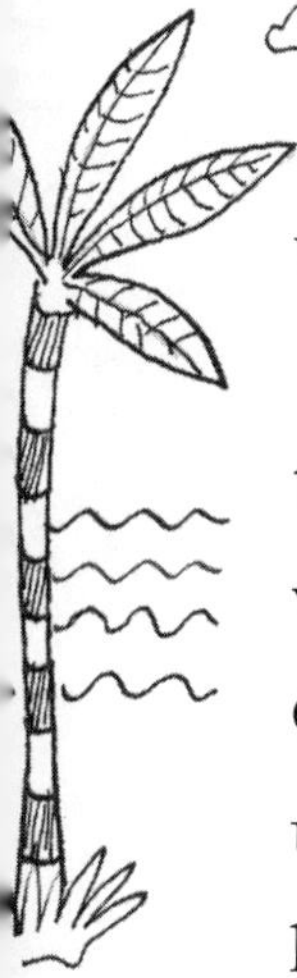
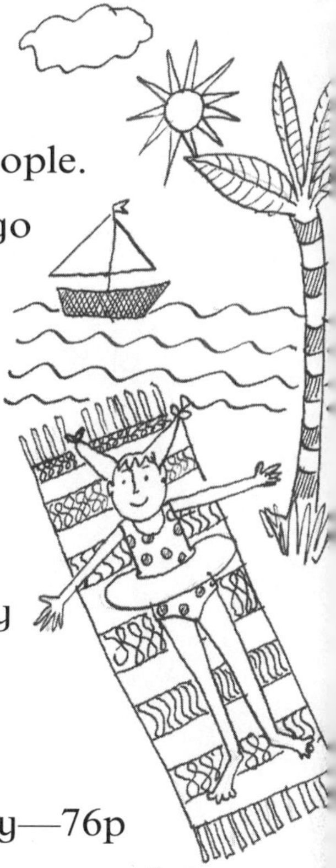

very polite to French people.

I would quite like to go to France again but I would prefer to go to Center Parks. It is very unfair not having a holiday because of a stupid baby that nobody wants anyway.

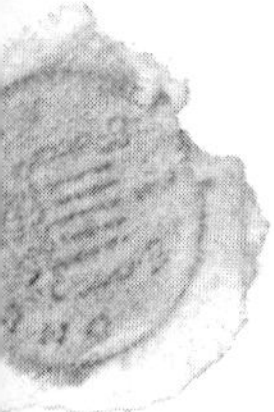

Horace—7 days

Running Away Money—76p

2 Double Deckers

1 sandwich

1 Snickers bar

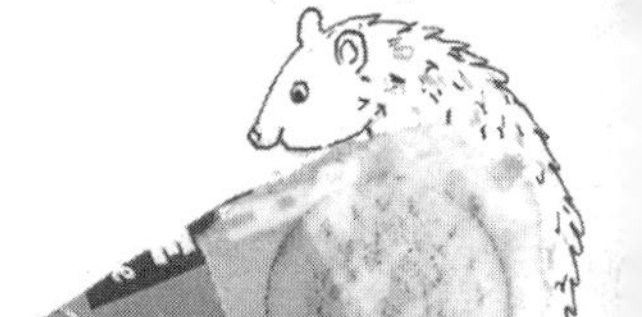
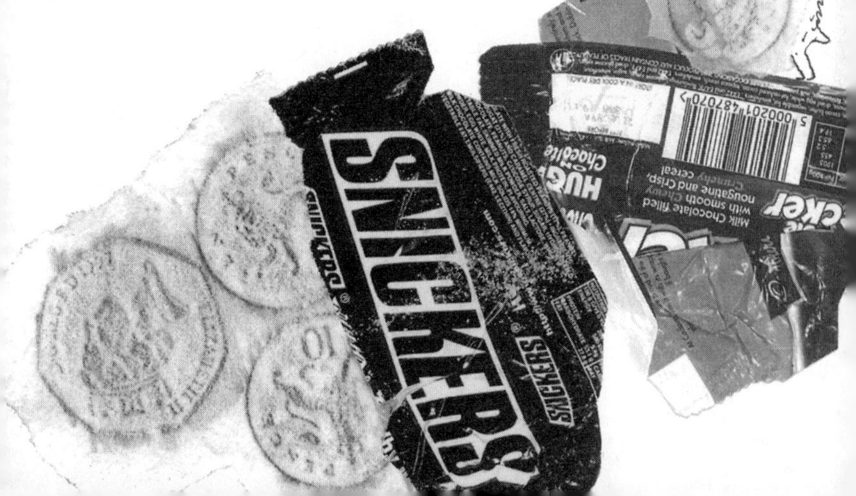
SNICKERS

Wednesday

Kelly and Lisa kept walking round the playground together. They were pretending to be sisters. They said, We're really sisters not pretend sisters.

Alex said, let's be sisters as well but I didn't want to. It is bad enough having a real sister.

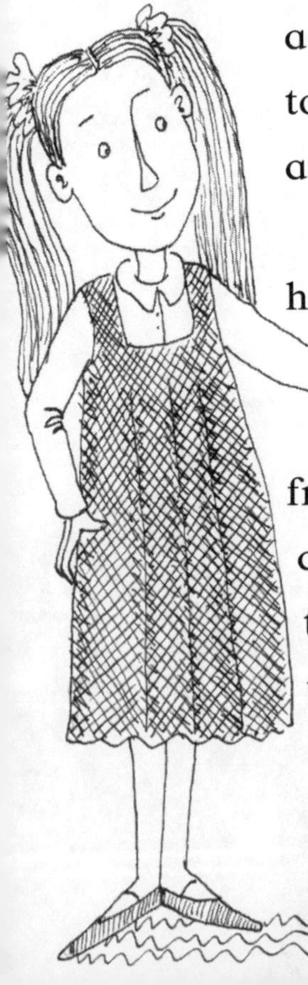

Kelly said I was not her best friend and I had never been her best friend because Lisa always always was. That is not true because she used to think Lisa was babyish.

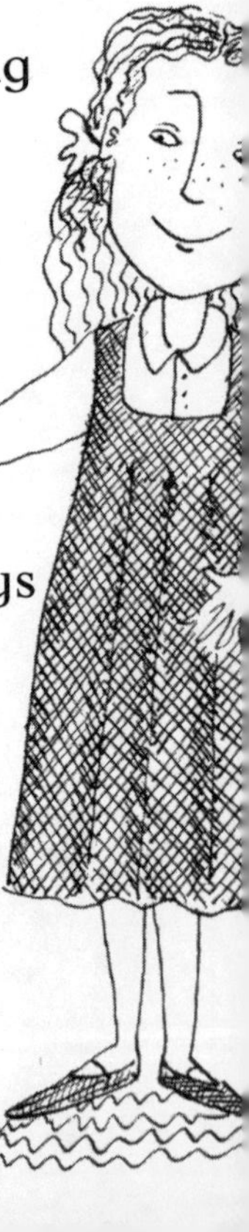

What's green and hairy and goes up and down?

A gooseberry in a lift.

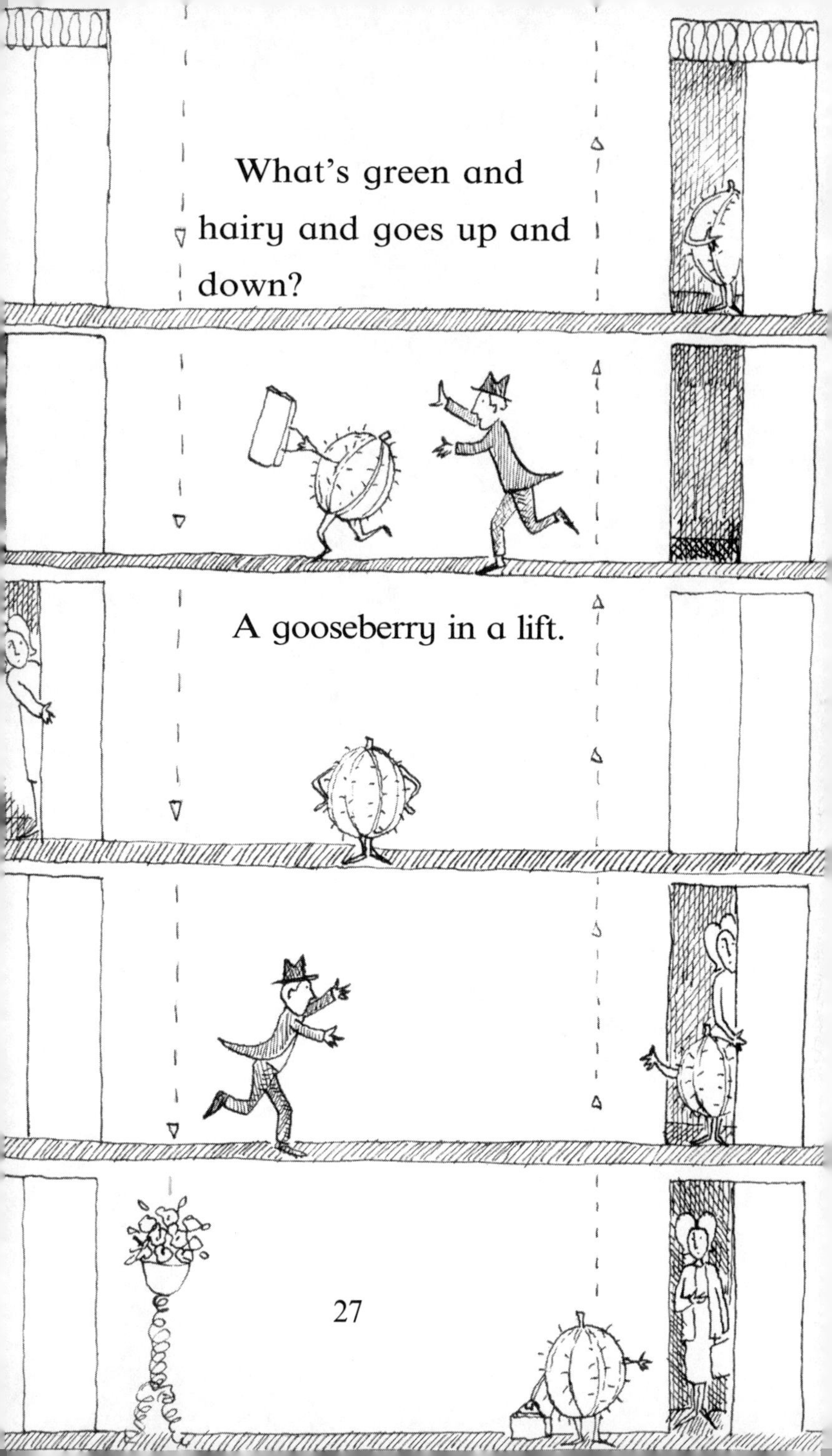

Why did the gooseberry cross the road?

I can't remember the answer to that one.

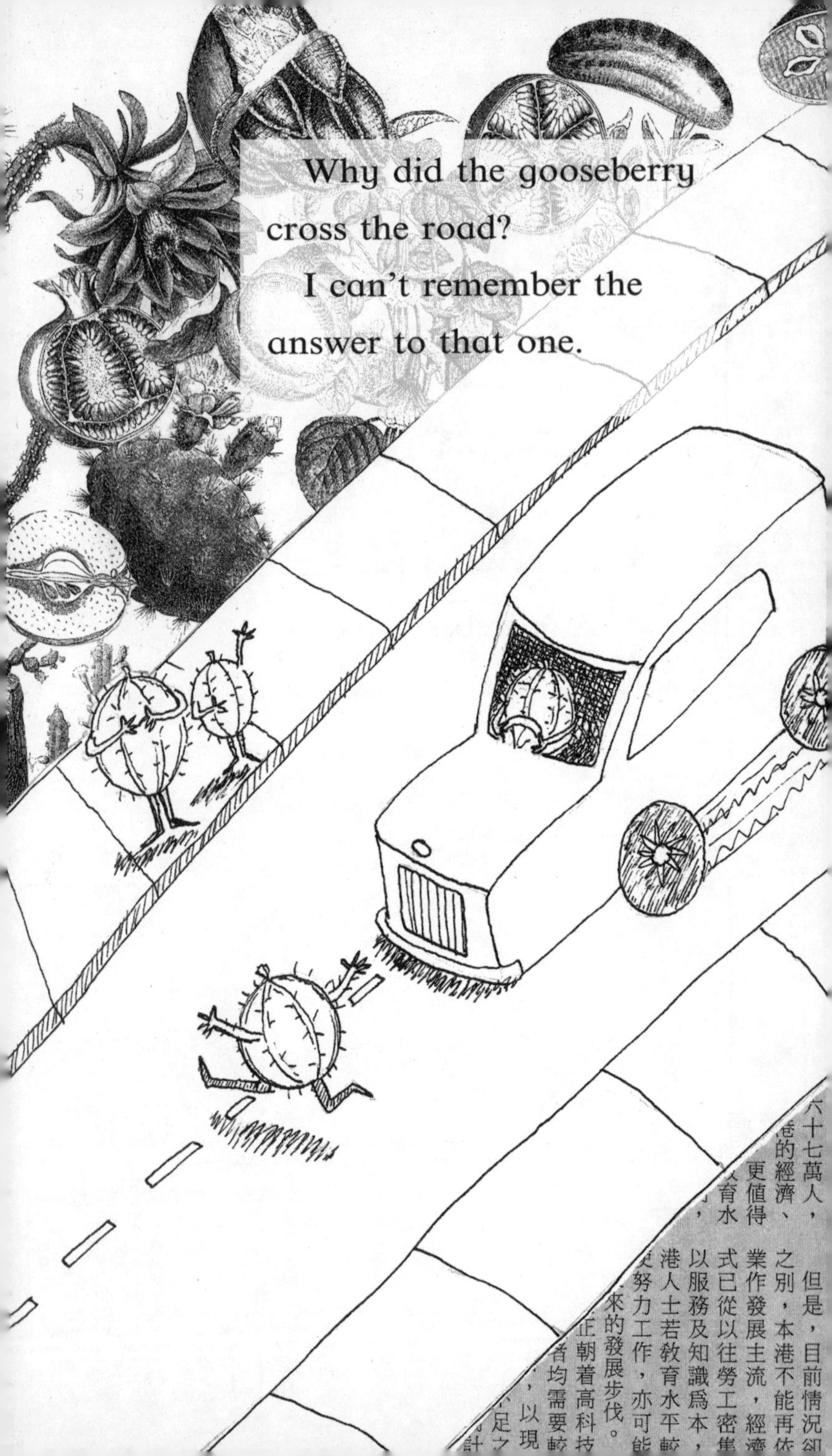

六十七萬人，
港的經濟、
更值得
教育水
但是，目前情況
之別，本港不能再依
業作發展主流，經濟
式已從以往勞工密集
以服務及知識為本，
港人士若教育水平較
努力工作，亦可能
來的發展步伐。
正朝着高科技
者均需要較

Saturday
THINGS I LIKE:
Crispy Duck
Prawn Toast

We went for a Chinese meal today. Mum said it might be the last chance before You-Know-Who.

There was a waiter there who kept singing. He was really funny. He held the tray on one hand and he sang I'm the King of the Swingers.

Chinese Toffee Apples are Yummy too. I used my chopsticks. It was great. Mopsy can't use

chopsticks. She had to have a spoon. Mum said she couldn't be doing with chopsticks. She had a fork. This is silly of her because chopsticks are the best.

Mopsy was a pain. She goes, this has got mushrooms, this has got lumpy bits.

Dad made his chopsticks do a dance on the table. Mopsy thought it was funny. Everyone else was looking at us. It was Inbarersing.

POCKET MONEY DAY!

Only I spent 50p on an orange Fruit Ice.

This was not very smart.

Horace—11 days

Running Away Money—

76p + £1 - 50p = £1.26

2 Double Deckers

1 sandwich

1 Snickers bar

Half a packet of chicken potato crisps—they are not very nice.

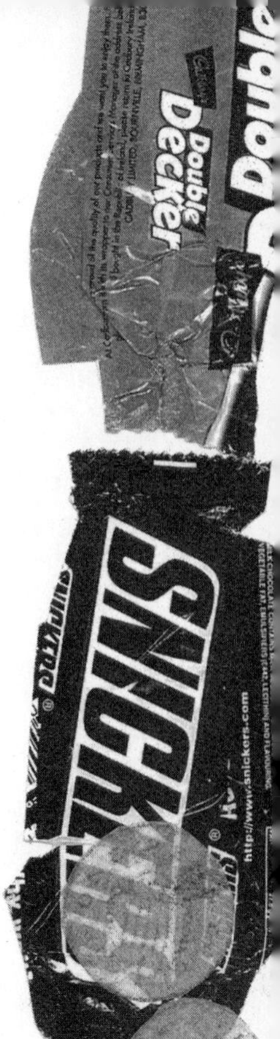
Double Decker
Double
http://www.snickers.com

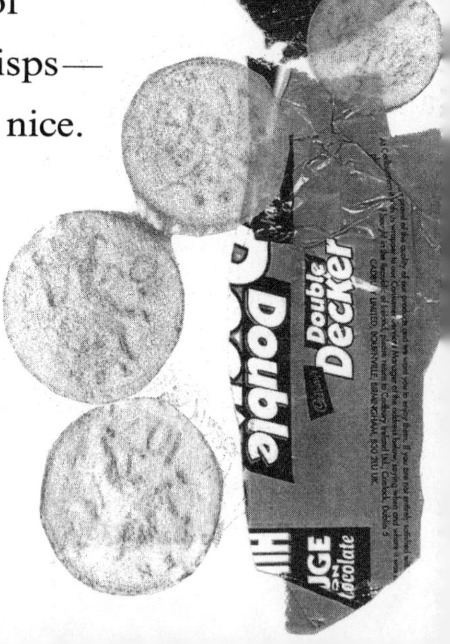
Double Decker
Double

Sunday

When Kelly goes to Disneyland she will have to speak French. She said, oh no I won't but she will. I am not going to tell her about pomfreet, so she will ask them for French fries and they won't know what she is on about.

Mrs. Fritwell came round. She is all skinny and her bracelets clank. She said she was doing a Bring-and-Buy for the

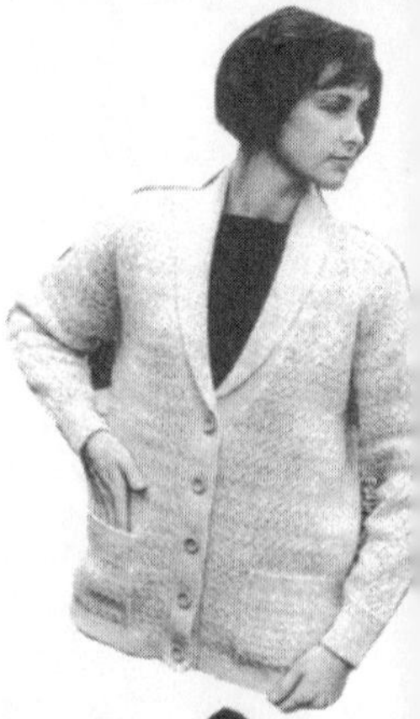

Children's Cruelty in July and would Mum do a stall.

Mum said she thought she'd have her hands full.

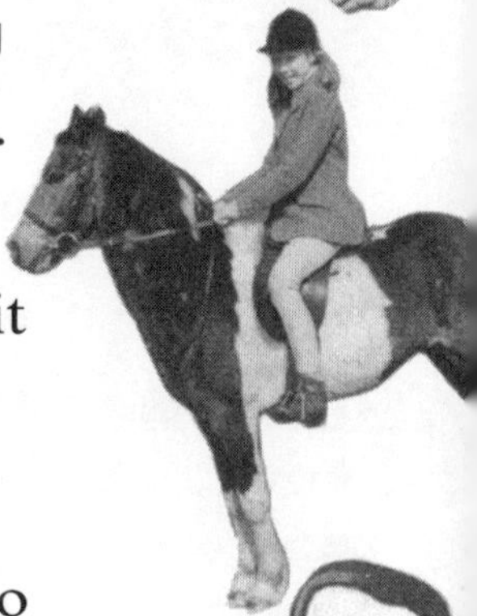

Mrs. Fritwell said, surely she'd be organized by July.

Mum said she was sorry but she'd rather not commit herself.

Mrs. Fritwell desided—oops—decided to have a go at me. She said, well Polly, are you looking forward to your New Baby?

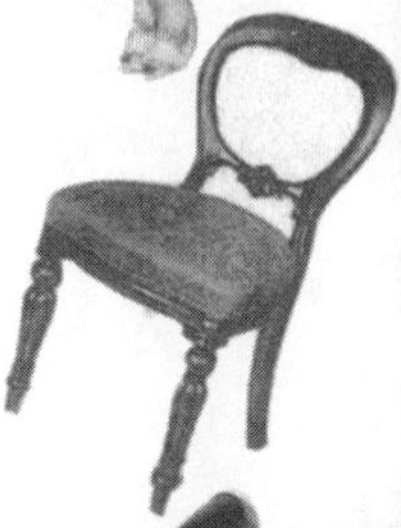

I said, no I'm not.

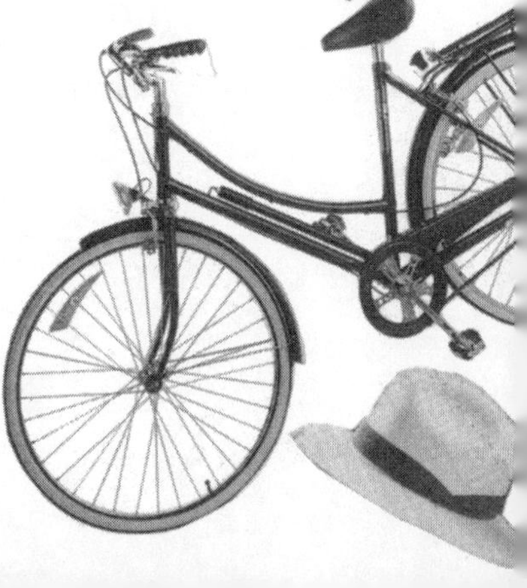

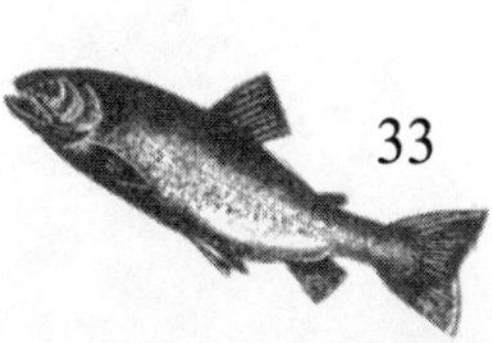

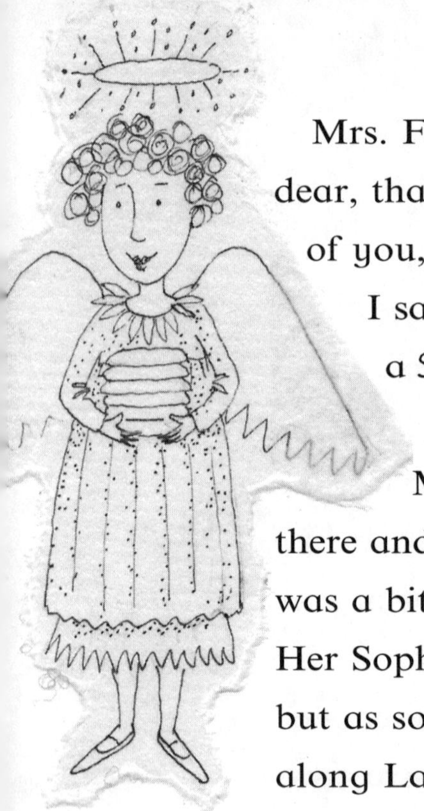

Mrs. Fritwell said, oh dear, that isn't very kind of you, is it?

I said, I'm going through a Stroppy Faze.

She looked at Mum like I wasn't there and said Her Laura was a bit like that when Her Sophie was on the way but as soon as Baby came along Laura was a Little Angel and used to fetch the diapers.

I was going to say, I'm not fetching diapers. But Mum started moving Mrs. Fritwell to the door and saying, so sorry, so kind

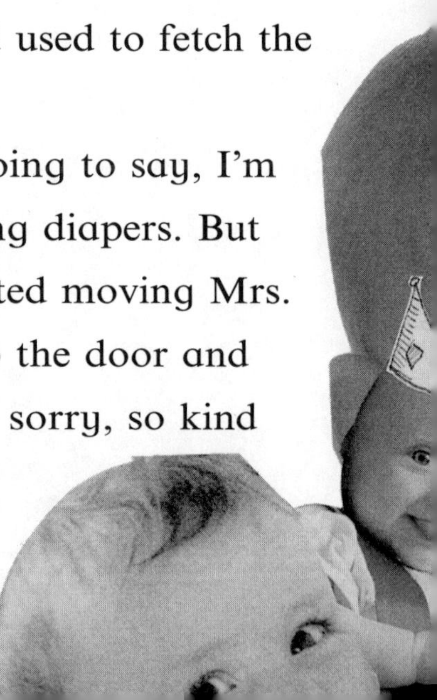

of you to think of me and we'd try to come to the Bring-and-Buy anyway.

I said we'll Bring the baby and hope someone Buys it.

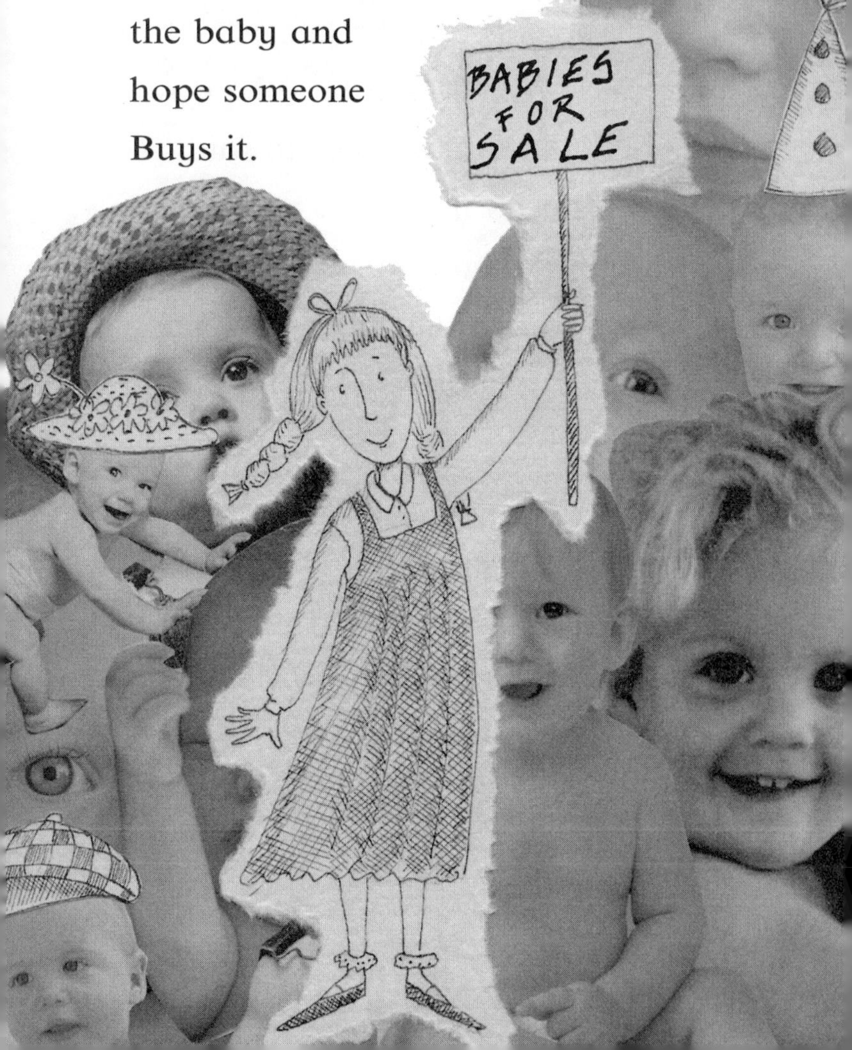
BABIES FOR SALE

Mum said, that's quite enough from you, Madam! I don't know what Mrs. Fritwell said, as she whispered it to Mum when she was out the door.

I asked Dad to write down pomfreet for me. He said, why do you want me to do that? I said, it's because I want to remember that I'm not going to tell Kelly what it is.

Dad said, I don't quite follow you, my darling, but I'll write it down for you.

Here is the bit of paper he wrote it on.

POMMES FRITES

It is still actually pomfreet and Kelly will not know how to say it.

I ate a Double Decker
Horace—12 days
£1.26
1 Double Decker
1 sandwich
1 Snickers bar

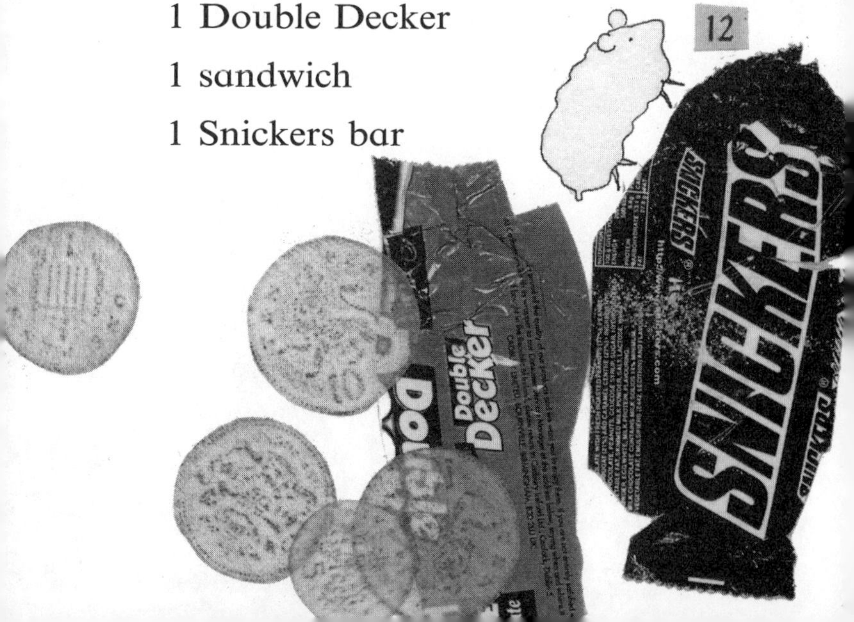
12
Double Decker
SNICKERS

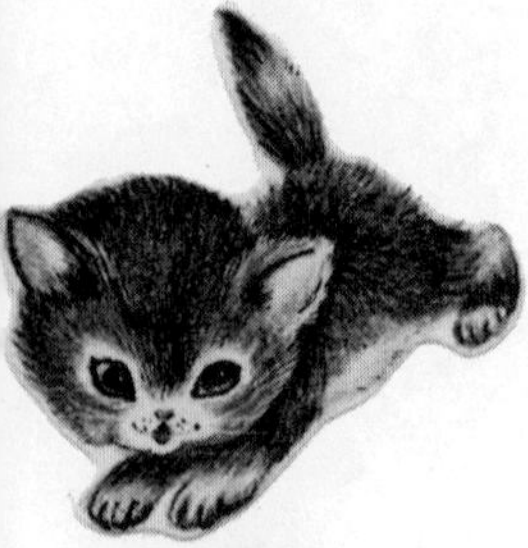

I did actually eat the potato crisps. There didn't seem much point in only half a packet.

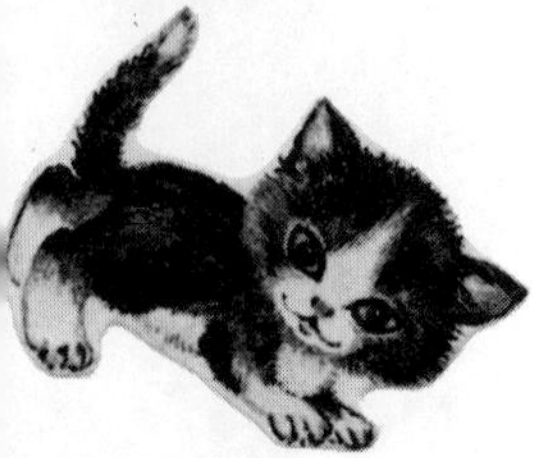

Snickers bars are very nice even though they have nuts. I am not Allergic to nuts, I just don't like them. Not as much as I don't like Brocerly.

I said to Mum, if Horace dies can we get a cat and she said, oh Polly, that doesn't sound very

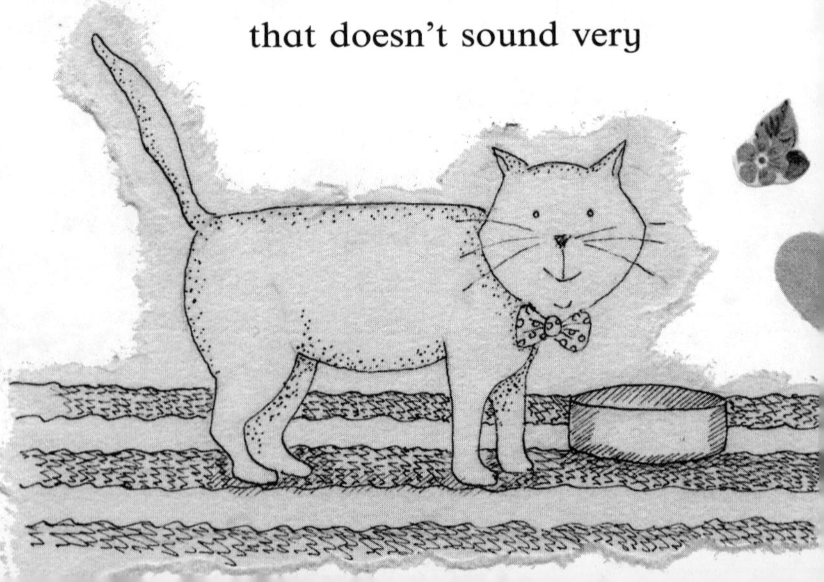

kind to poor Horace. And I said, yes but can we. She said, no dear, she didn't think so because cats are a nuisance when you go on holiday. I said, but according to Dad we aren't having a holiday anyway. I said it in a sarcastic voice but it was a complete waste of being sarcastic because she just said, yes but they're a nuisance anyway and could I be an angel and fetch the scissors from the kitchen drawer.

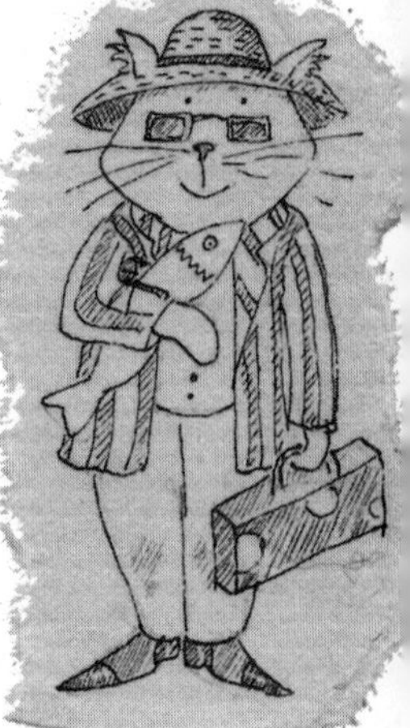

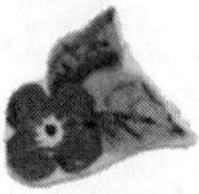

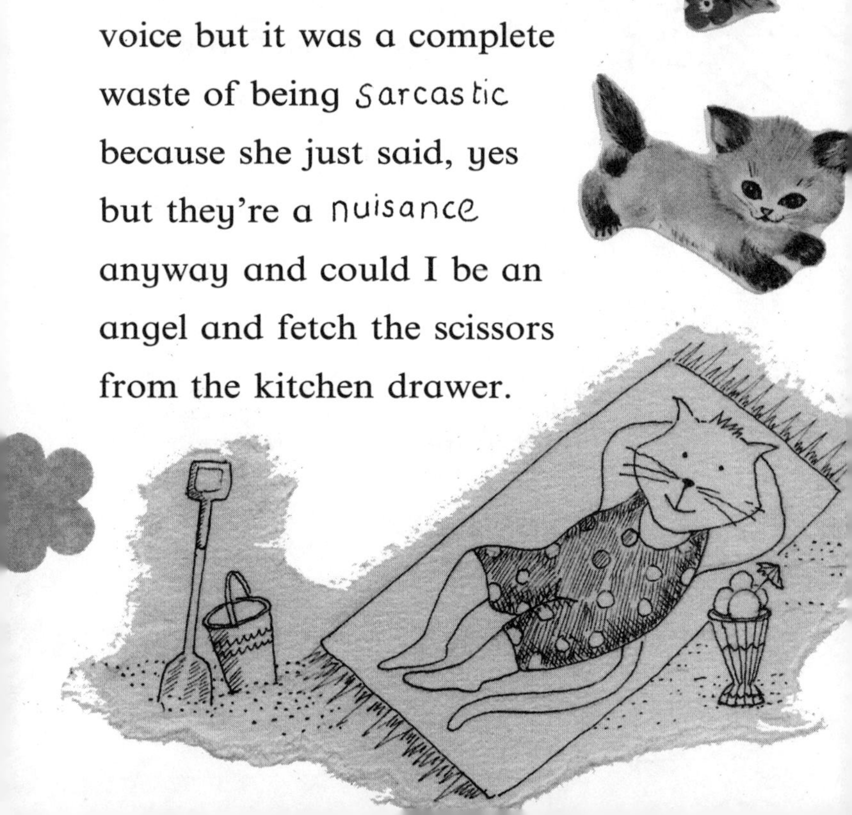

Date..........

Monday

We had Diary in school. I wrote about Dad and the chopsticks. Miss Price said, that isn't very nice when poor Daddy is trying to be nice to you, and anyway it is spelt Embarrassing. I don't think People should be Embarrassing, specially parents.

We did Queen Elizabeth in the Tudors. Queen Elizabeth was very grand. She liked to dance. She had lots of palaces. When she was old she wore a red wig.

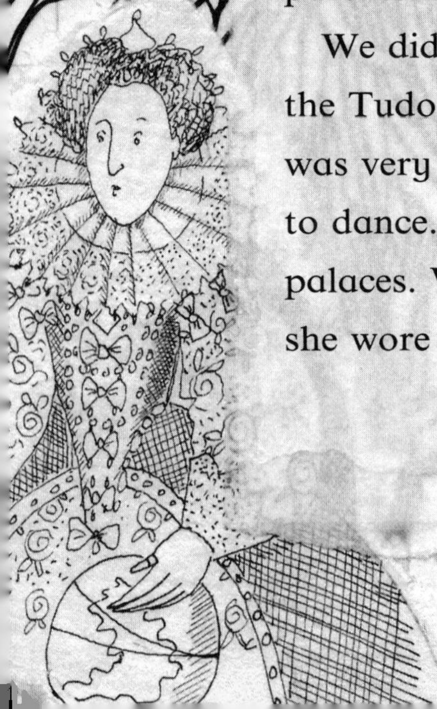

I said, did she throw her poo out of the window too?

Miss Price said, probably it was only the poor people who did that, the rich people had someone to do it for them, and could we please talk about something else.

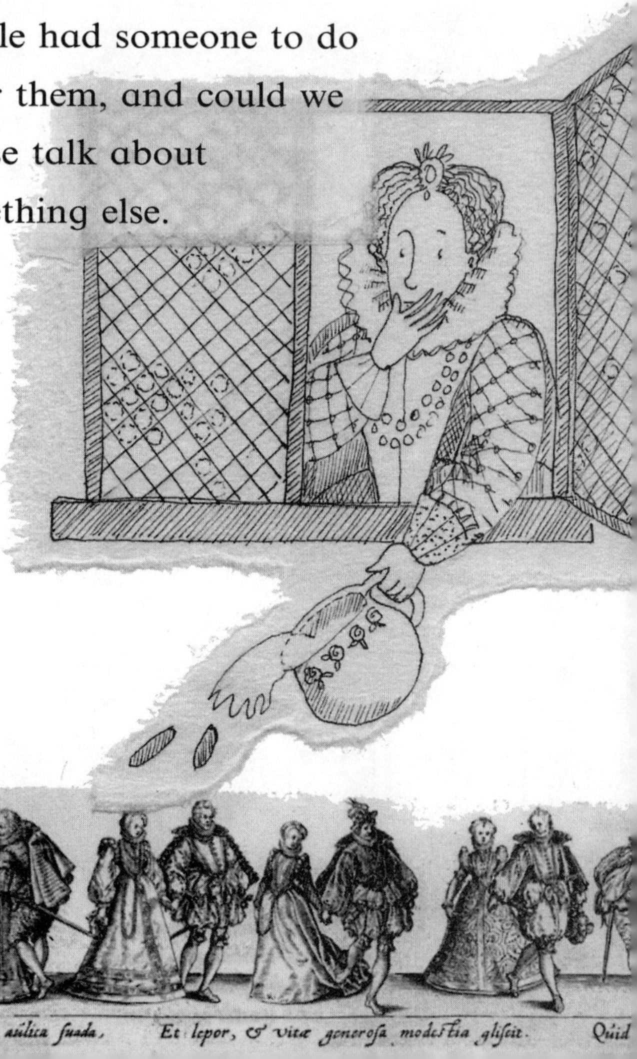
Et lepor, & vitæ generosa modestia glisçit.

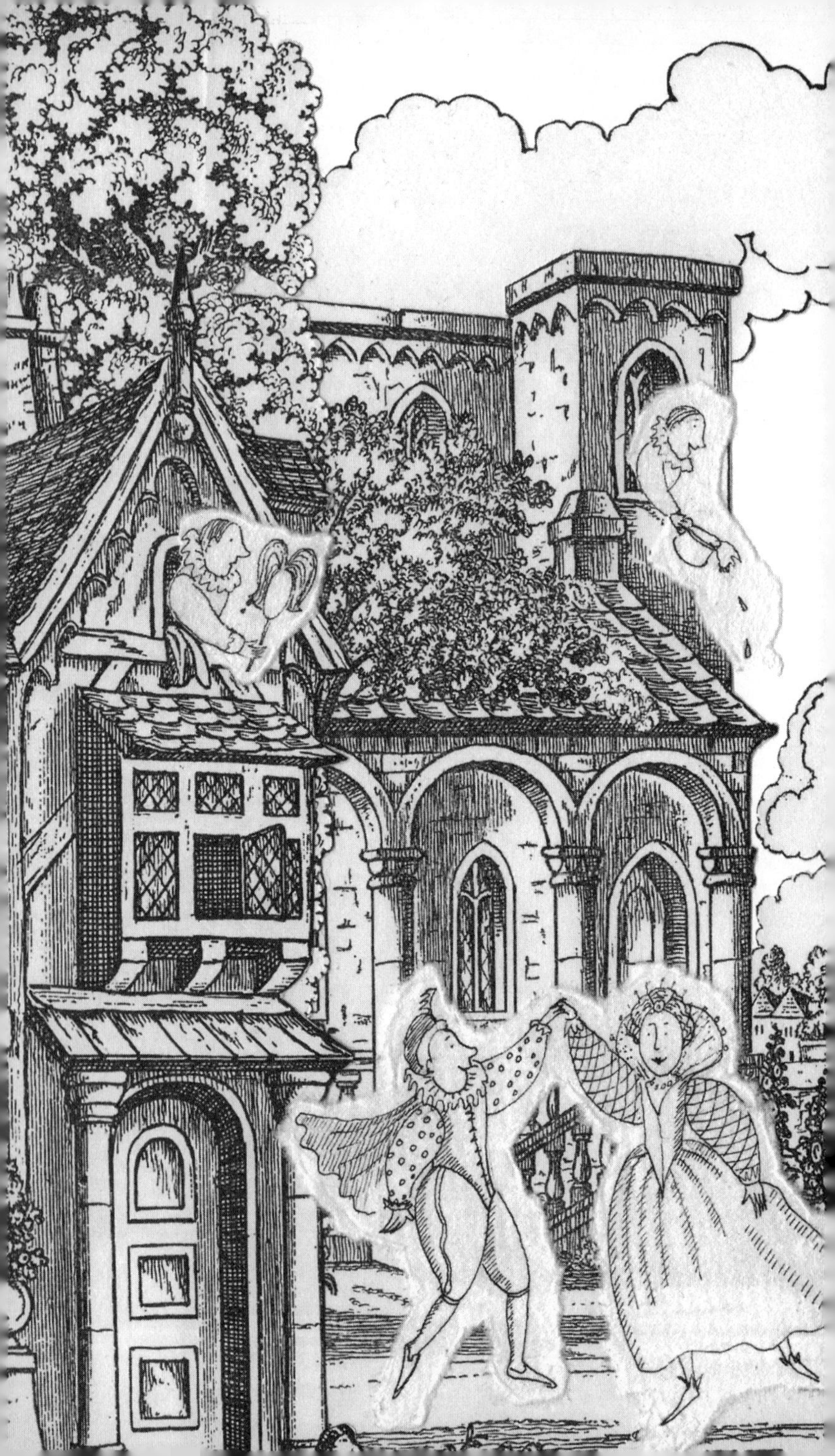

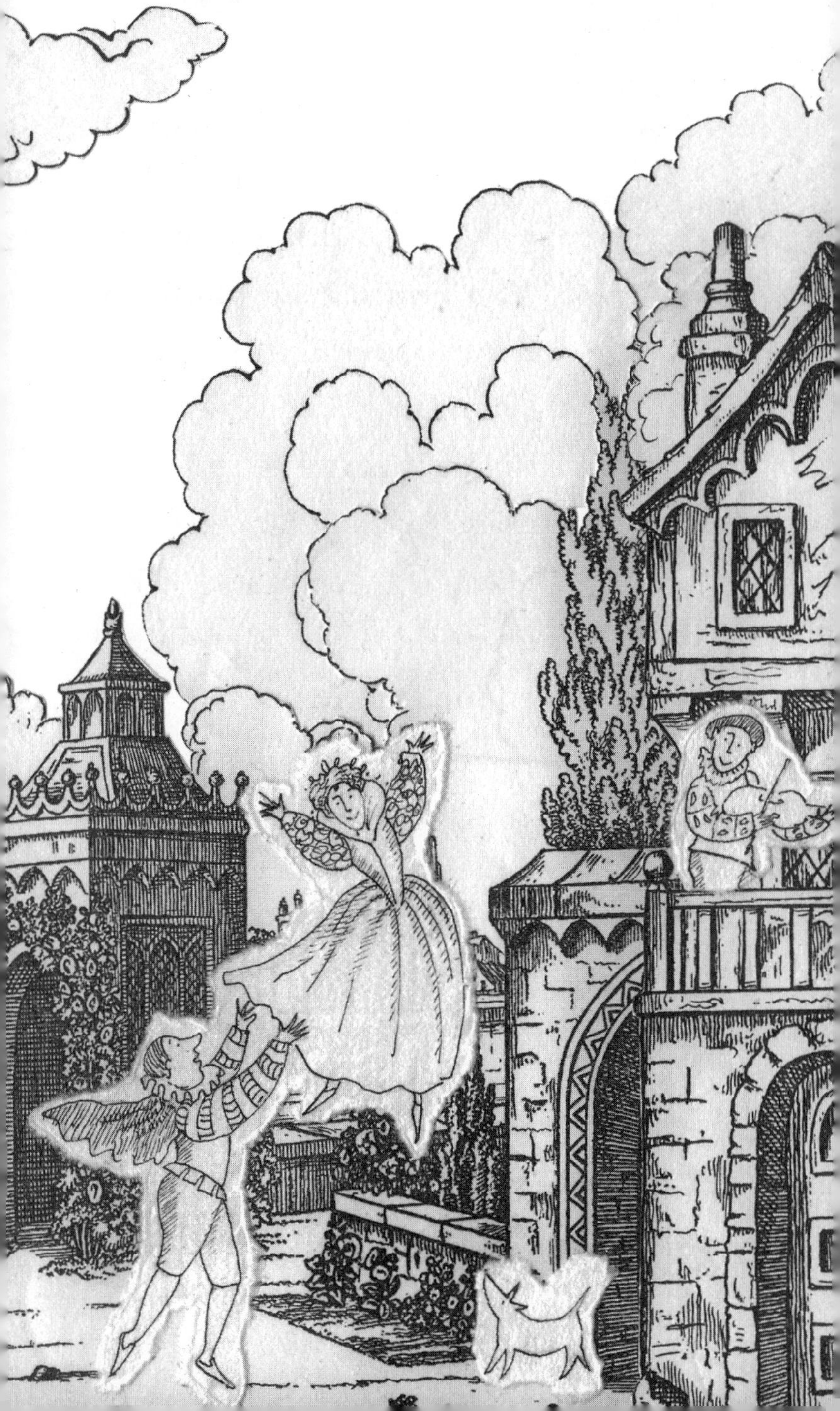

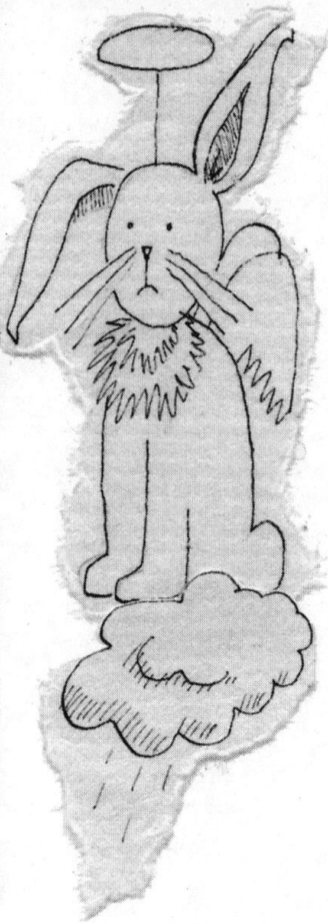

Alex is silly. She says when she is grown up she will be like Britney Spears. You mustn't say Fluffy to her because Fluffy was her rabbit that died. Every time you say Fluffy she cries. But I think she is just doing it to get noticed. I don't think she is really crying.

Also she says her mum lets her watch television all day which is silly because nobody does.

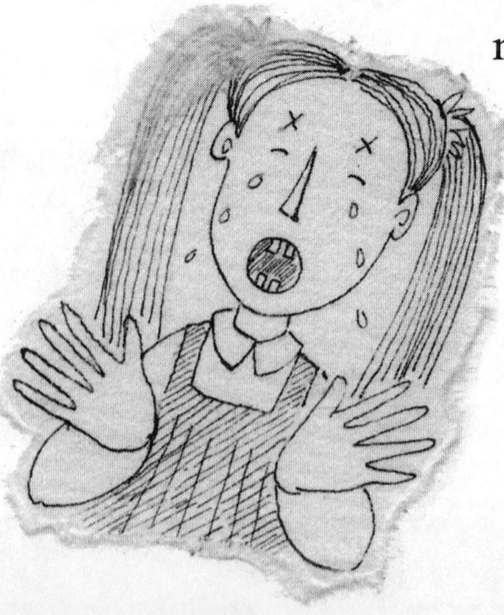

I liked Kelly better when she was being my best friend.

She is still going to Disneyland. She said she might send me a postcard.

Tuesday

Mrs. Muldoon was in one of her moods. She told us all off this morning for:

1) running up the stairs.

2) being rude to the dinner ladies (this is not fair. It was only Darren who was rude to the dinner ladies. He said that the chicken pie was really dead mouse pie. The rest

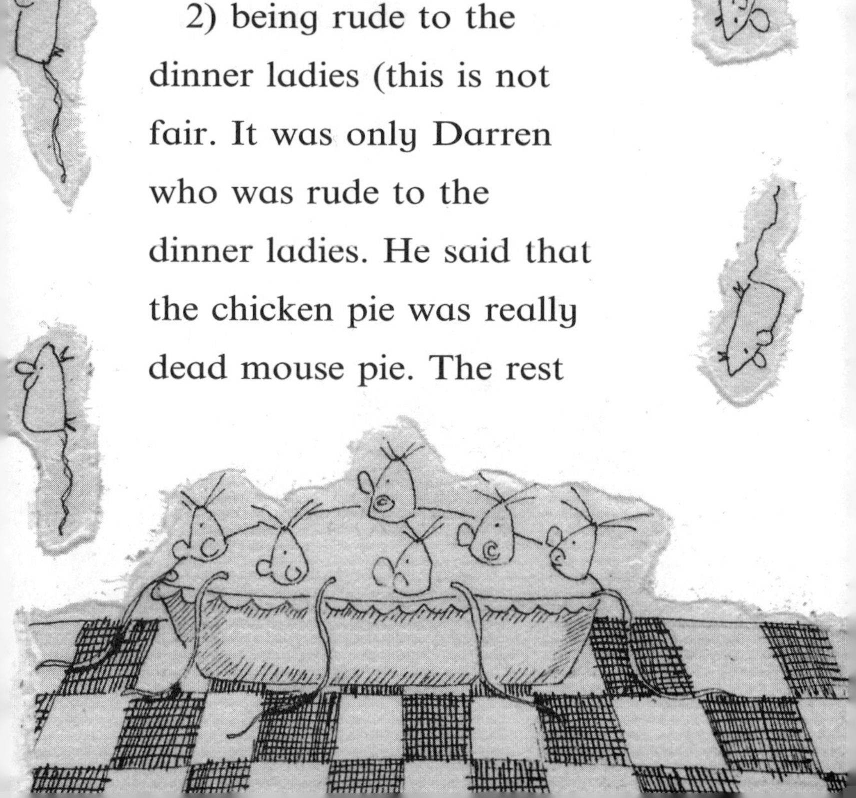

of us are <u>never</u> rude to the dinner ladies even though they are sometimes quite rude to us).

3) not playing proper games in the playground. She said all we do is Hang around and we should learn to skip like she did when she was a little girl.

a b c d e f g h

Yes, and I bet they used to throw their poo out of the windows too when she was a little girl.

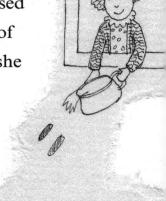

Katy Poole's mum is a friend of Mrs. Muldoon. She says that Mrs. Muldoon's son Paul smokes twenty sigarets a day and will not make his bed. Mrs. Muldoon gets very cross with him which is why she takes it out on us.

Miss Price is not going to marry Nigel. He is not her best friend anymore. She says, can we just shut up about it, please. I suppose it is Embarrassing her. But we have to talk about Embarrassing things, so why not her?

I said to Lee—not Center Parks Lee who was a girl but my class Lee who is a boy—I said, why is Six afraid of Seven? Because Seven Eight Nine. I said, do you get it, and he said yes.

Then I heard him telling Charlie the joke. He goes,

8

6

86

0

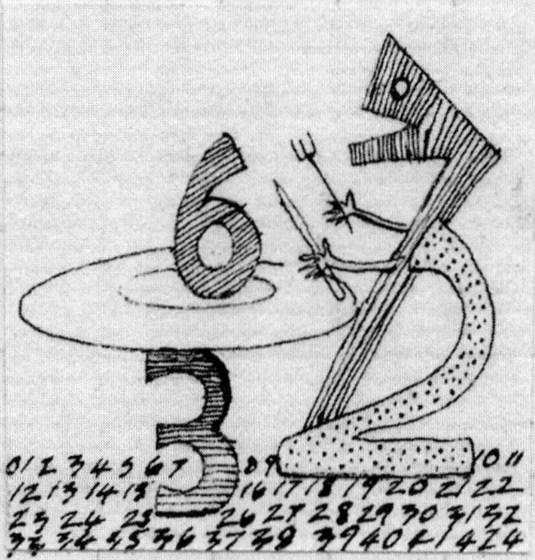

3

7

4

18

40

3 4 5 6 7 8 9 10 11 12 13 14 15 16 17 18 19 20 21 22 23 24 25 26 27 28

79

5

1

4

Over 600

147

28

9

GUANGHWA COMPANY

£1.00

32 PARKER STREET WC2

0171-831 5888

Why is Eight afraid of
Nine? Because Eight Nine
Ten.

Really really stupid.

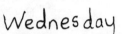

Wednesday

Darren said Horace had
probably been eaten by a
fox because they had a fox
in their street and it ate
everyone's rabbits. Alex
cried because he said
rabbits. He didn't even say
Fluffy. This is getting
really stupid.

I don't think Horace has
been eaten by a fox.

Today we did

50

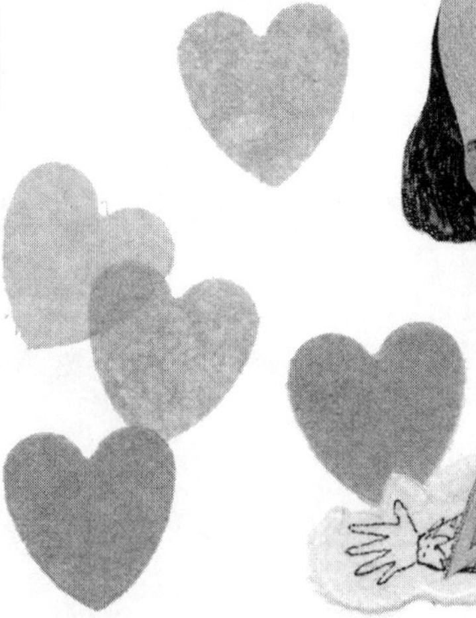

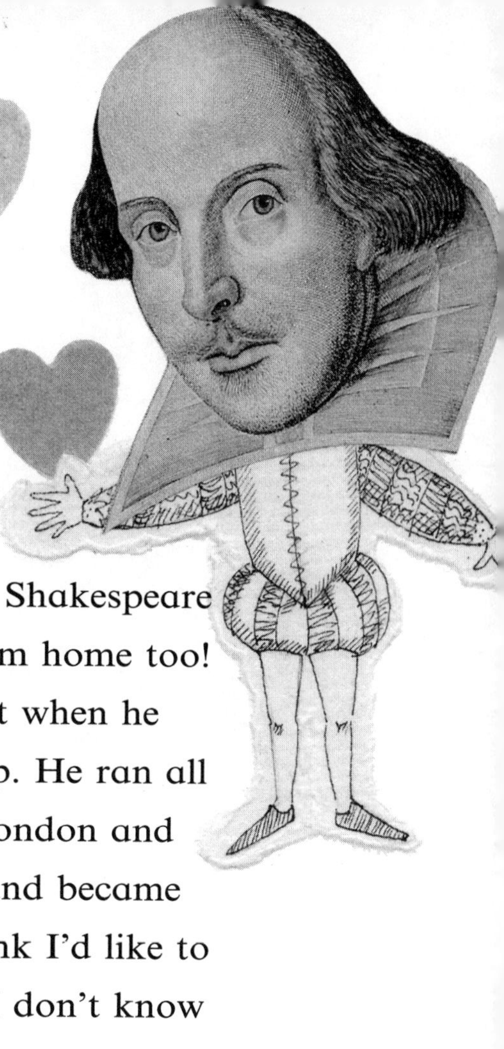

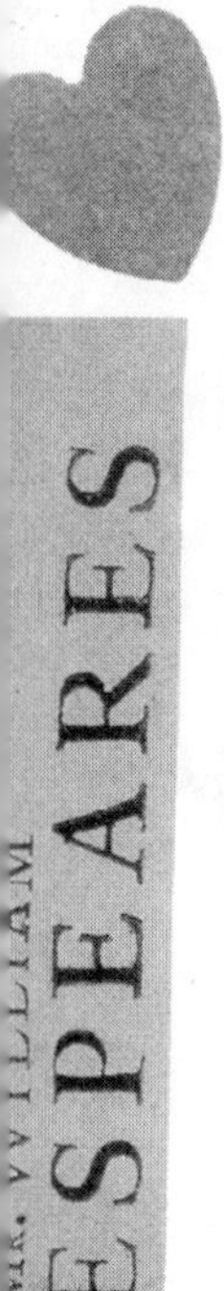
SHAKESPEARES

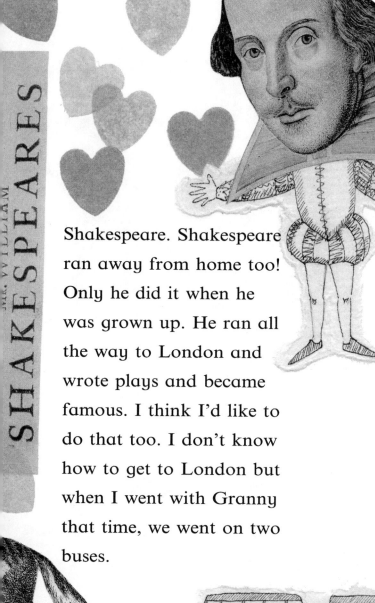

Shakespeare. Shakespeare ran away from home too! Only he did it when he was grown up. He ran all the way to London and wrote plays and became famous. I think I'd like to do that too. I don't know how to get to London but when I went with Granny that time, we went on two buses.

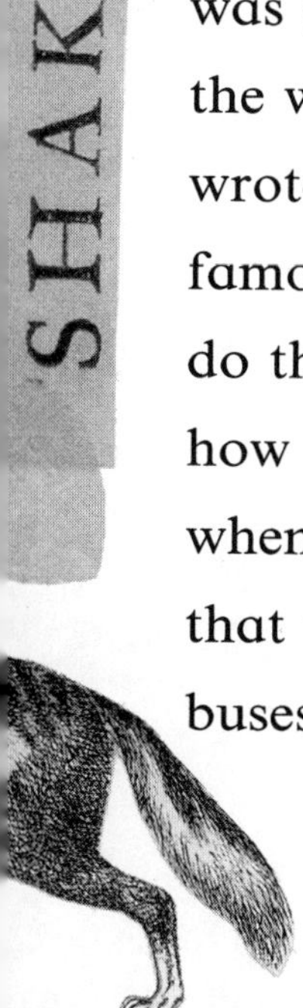

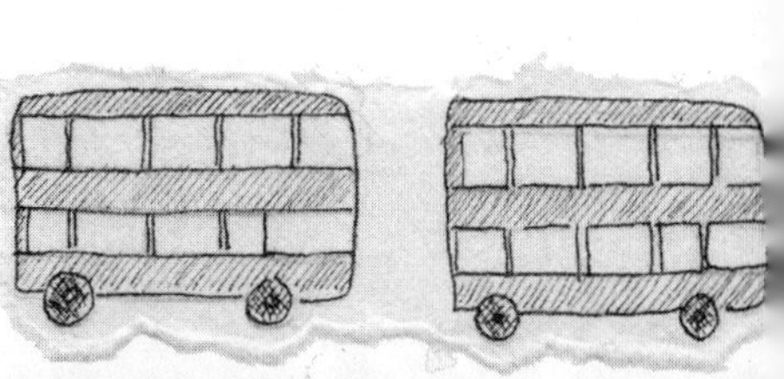

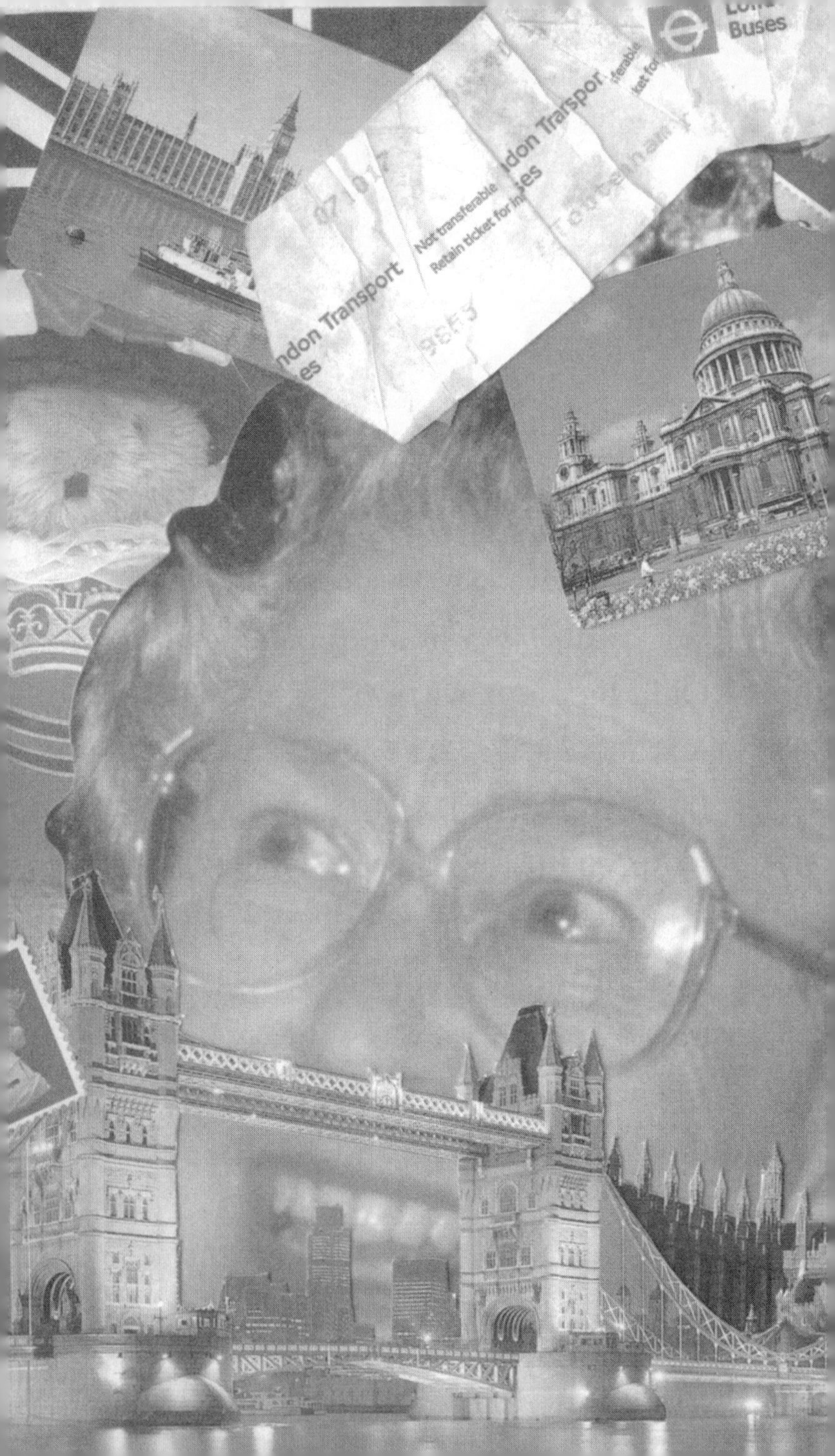
Buses
Not transferable

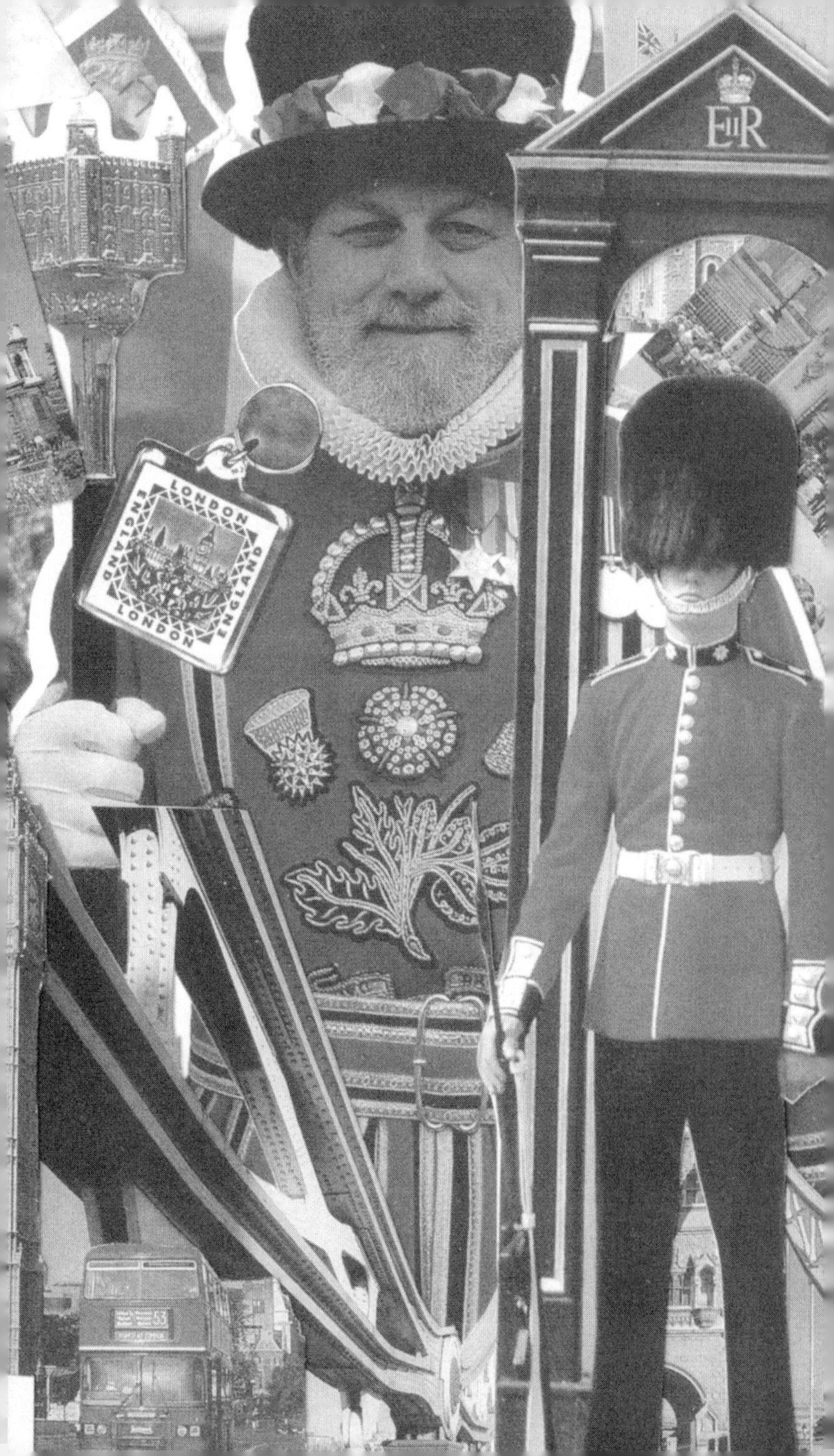
EIIR
LONDON
ENGLAND
LONDON
ENGLAND

We did Silent Letters in spelling. K now. K nife. K nack. I think they are silly. I said, why did we have to have Silent Letters and Miss Price said, I don't know dear, I didn't invent the Rules. I said, suppose everyone said one day let's not have any more Silent Letters—then they wouldn't have to have them and we wouldn't have to do them. Miss Price said it didn't work that way. But if you are a Grown Up why can't you just say no Silent Letters. Nobody likes them. They are really dumb.

Dumb has a silent letter
too. Dumb, Thumb.
Darren said Dumb,
Thumb, Bum, and Miss P
said, No dear, not Bum,
and can we not be rude
all the time.

Also: Big Elephants
Can't Always Use Small
Entrances.

Pink Elephants On Pills
Laugh Easily.

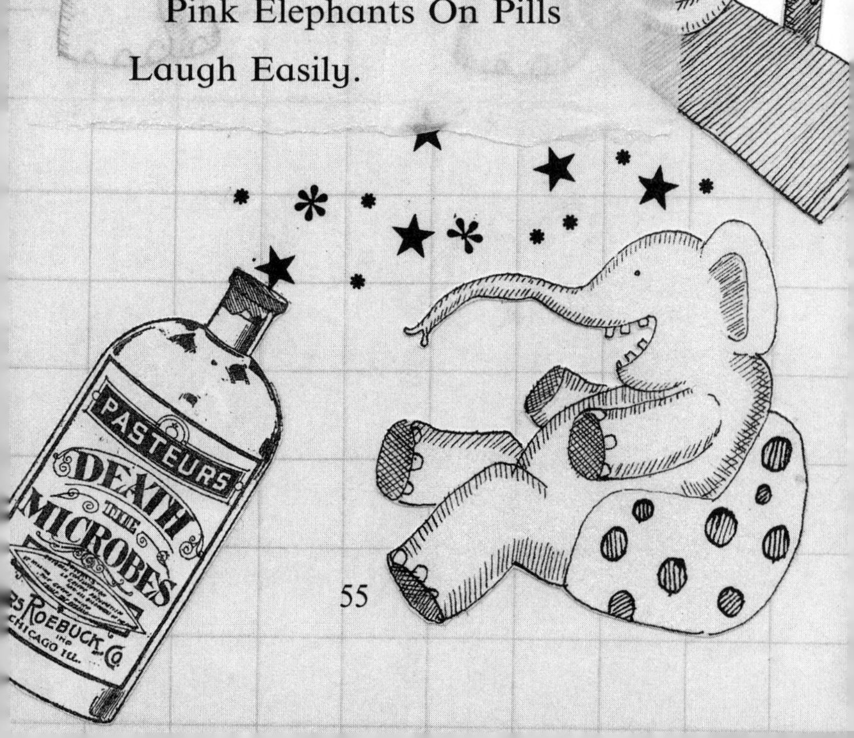
PASTEURS
DEATH
THE
MICROBES
ROEBUCK & Co
CHICAGO ILL.

ANNOYING THINGS
ABOUT KELLY:

1. She is going on and on about Disneyland.

2. She is not my best friend.

3. Powerpuff Girls is her best program.

4. Her new haircut is too short at the back. It makes her ears look all big.

She has very big ears anyway.

Shakespeare died on his birthday. That is so sad.

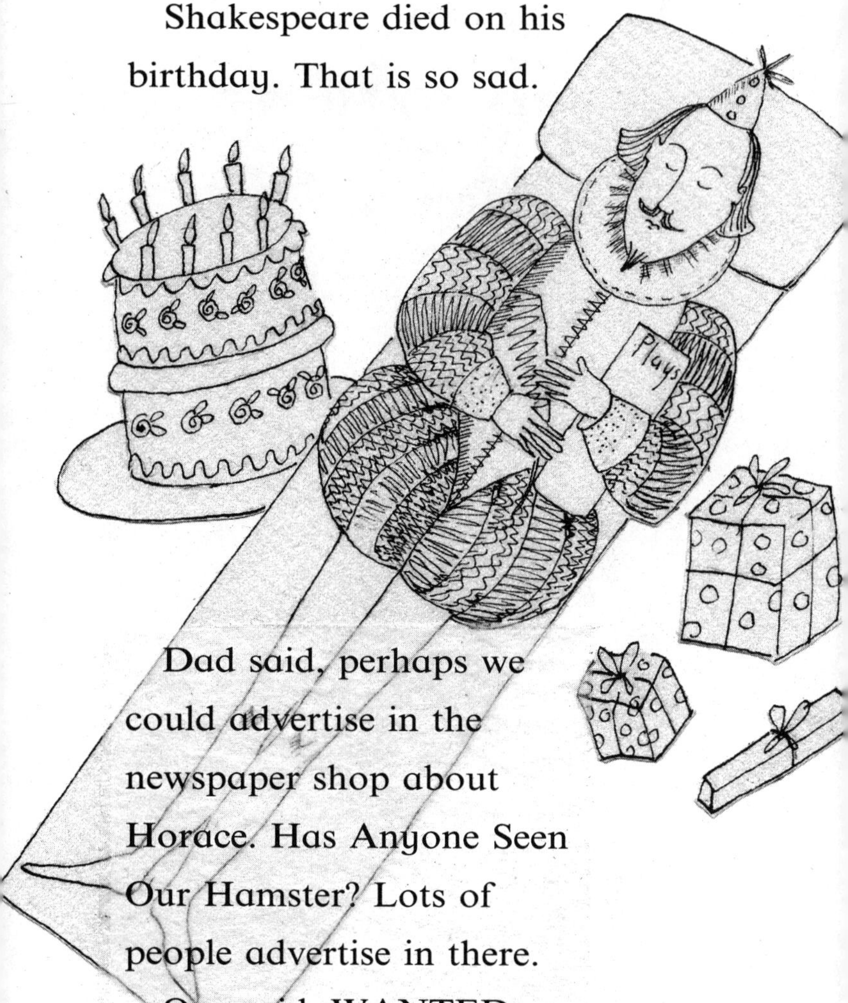
Plays

Dad said, perhaps we could advertise in the newspaper shop about Horace. Has Anyone Seen Our Hamster? Lots of people advertise in there.

One said, WANTED: child's bicycle, any

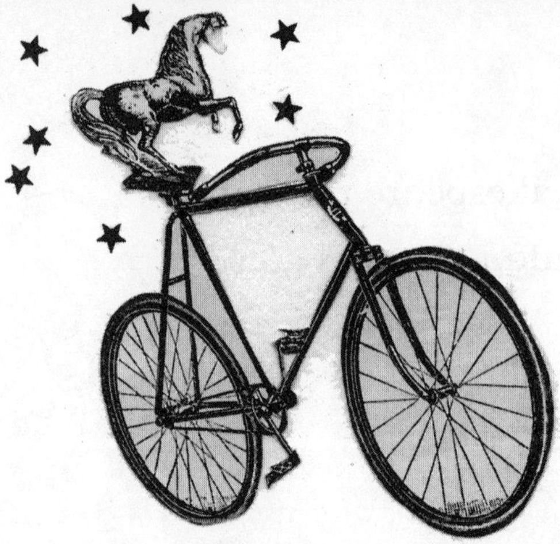

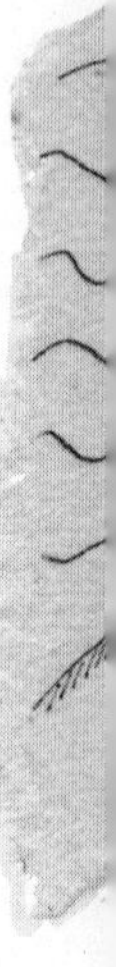

condition. Dad said, I bet that poor child doesn't want his bicycle in any condition.

I could advertise for a family. WANTED: proper family for nice girl, any condition.

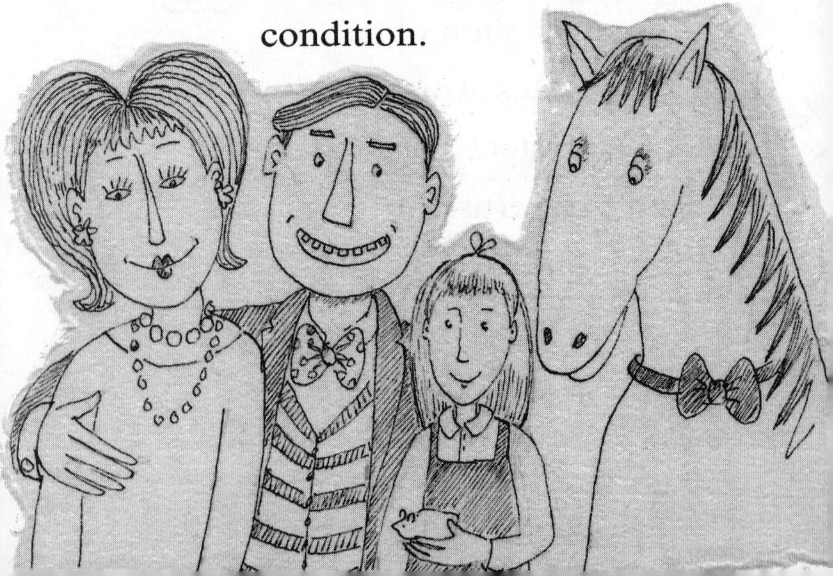

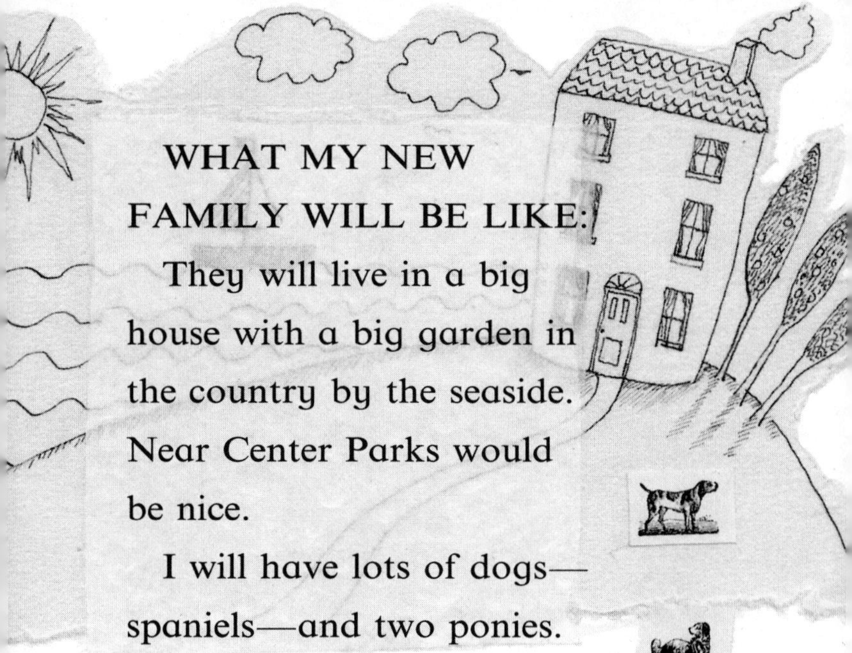

WHAT MY NEW FAMILY WILL BE LIKE:

They will live in a big house with a big garden in the country by the seaside. Near Center Parks would be nice.

I will have lots of dogs—spaniels—and two ponies. My ponies will be called Brandy and Danielle.

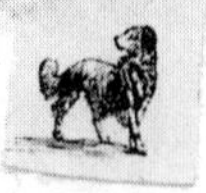

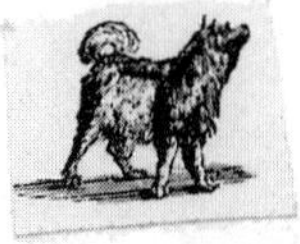

I WON'T HAVE SISTERS!!! OR BABIES!!!

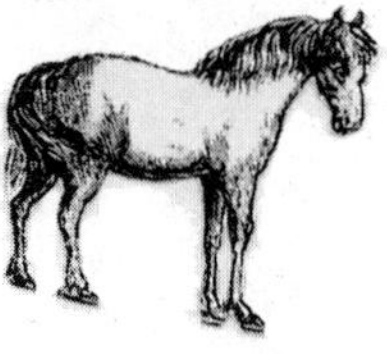

My dad will not be inbarasing embarrassing.

My mum will have an interesting job in a toy shop or a candy shop.

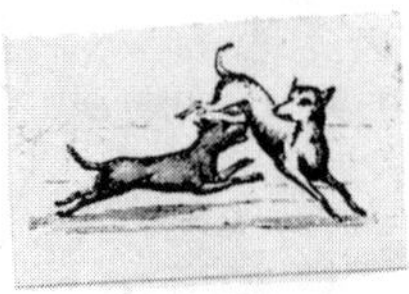

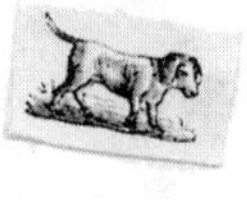

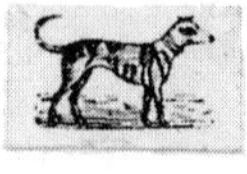

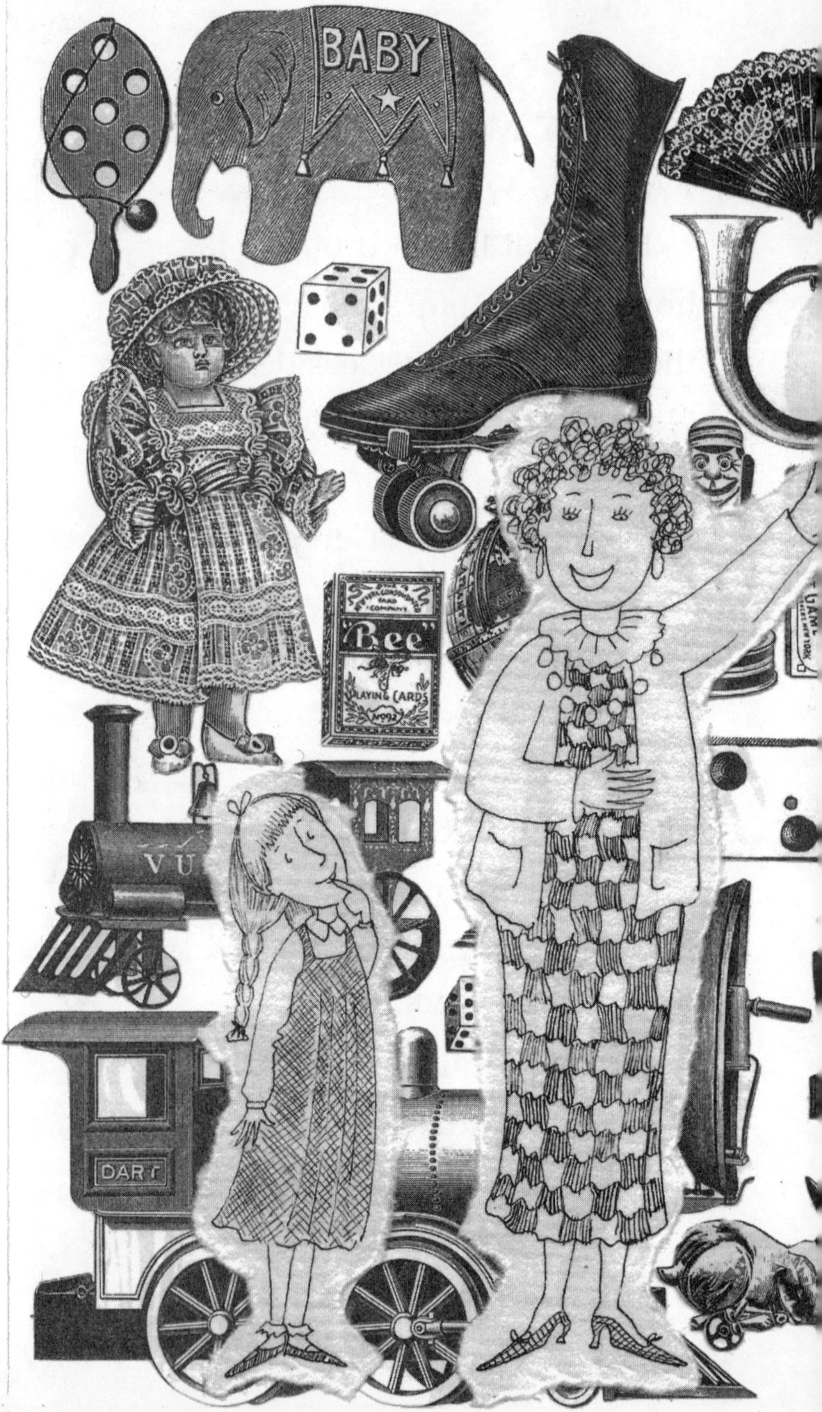
BABY
"Bee"
PLAYING CARDS
DART

She will not make
brocerly.

I will change my name to

Thursday

Last night they were
moving about and
whispering. Dad came in
and said, are you asleep,
Poll? I pretended to be and
he said, it's all right, she's
dead to the world.

In the morning, Granny
was there. I said, where's
Mum?

She said, Mummy's gone
to the hospital.

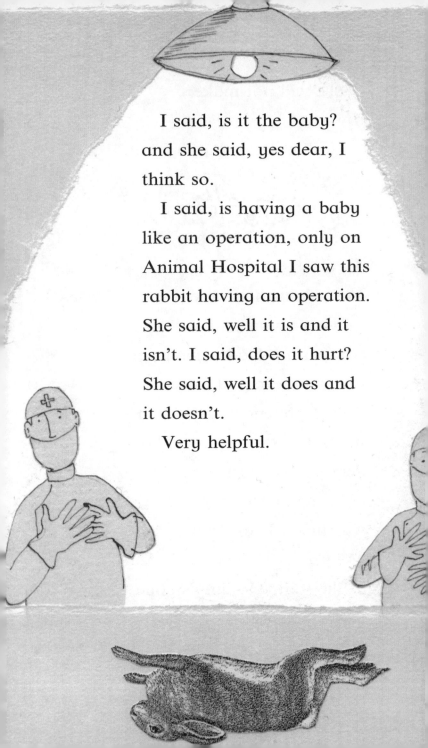

I said, is it the baby?
and she said, yes dear, I
think so.

I said, is having a baby
like an operation, only on
Animal Hospital I saw this
rabbit having an operation.
She said, well it is and it
isn't. I said, does it hurt?
She said, well it does and
it doesn't.

Very helpful.

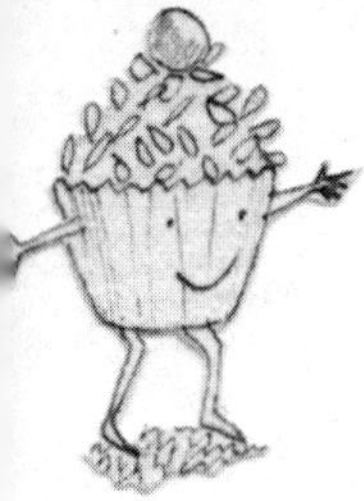

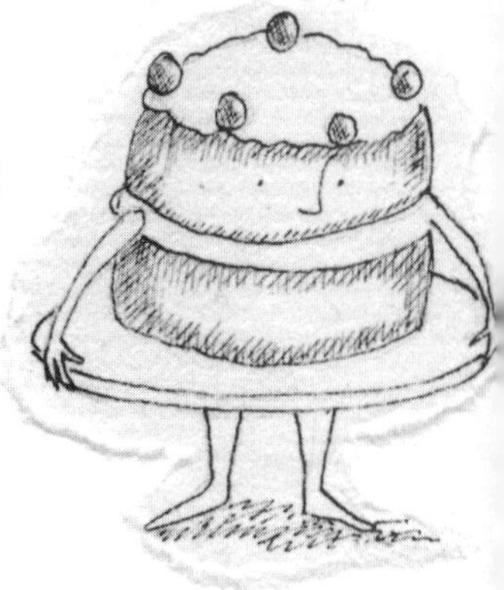

She said, look, hasn't your mummy told you all about these things and maybe you should ask her.

I said, how can I ask her, she's in the hospital.

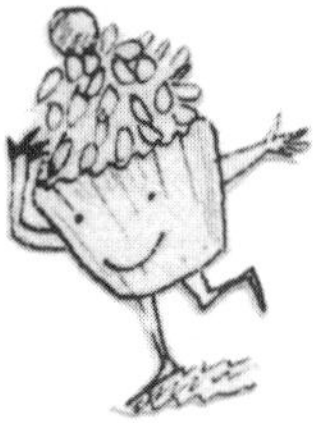

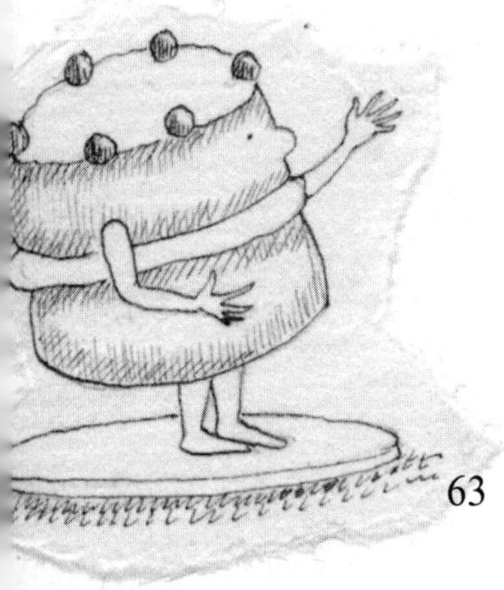

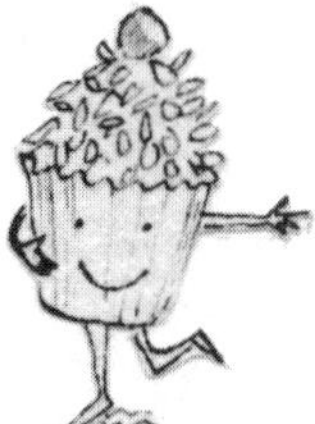

Granny said, how
about if we didn't go to
school today?

I said, what about the
Tudors?

Granny said she thought
one day didn't matter and
we could make some cakes.

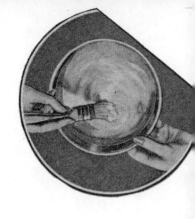

I said, the chocolate ones
with Rice Krispies, and she
said, oh no, that's far too
easy, I'll show you how to
make real cakes.

Grannies are peculiar.

I said I heard a scratchy noise in the bathroom and could it be Horace?

She said I must be imagining things.

They always say that.

I expect Granny would give me some money for Running Away as long as I didn't tell her what it was for.

We watched Teletubbies. We made cakes. Mopsy said they had lumpy bits and wouldn't eat them. Granny said, all the more for us. I like the ones with Rice Krispies better but I

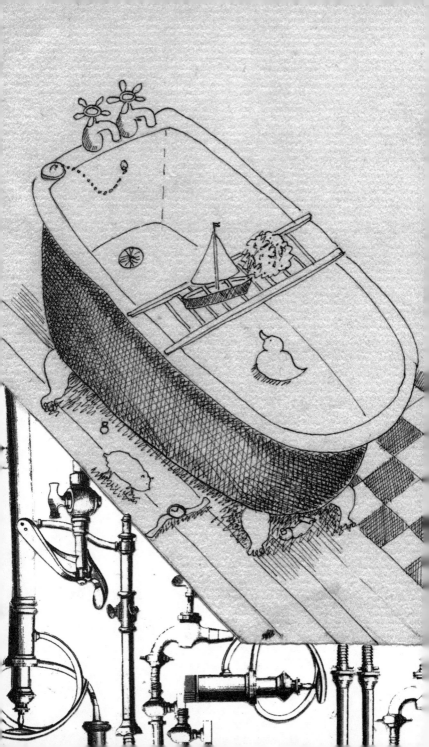

didn't say as I am much more politer than Mopsy.

Dad phoned from the hospital. He said everything was going well and give a big hug to his two Princesses.

This is quite boring really. I wish I was at school.

My sandwich has gone blue. I had to throw it away.

We had just put on the cartoons when the phone rang again. Granny went to pick it up.

She was going: Oooh! Oooh! Oooh! Wonderful.

She said, I must tell the girls.

She said, you have a little baby brother!

Mopsy said, Yippee, yippee!

I said, did Dad know?

She said, that was Daddy on the phone, silly.

I said, when did we have to see the baby?

She said she wasn't sure but maybe in a day or two

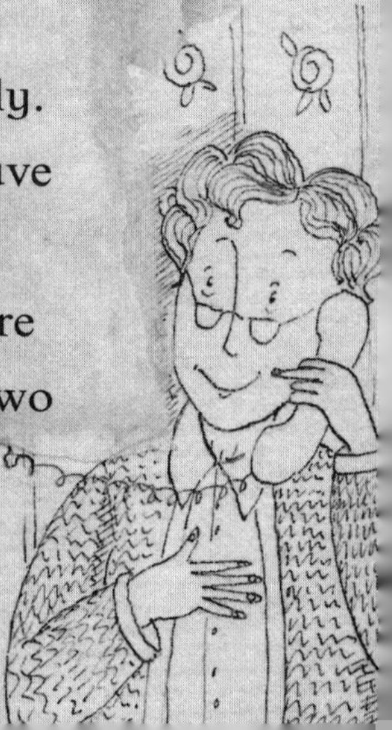

and what did we want for supper?

I said, could we have Take-Away Pizza.

Mopsy said, I don't like Pizza.

Granny said, maybe they could make you a special one.

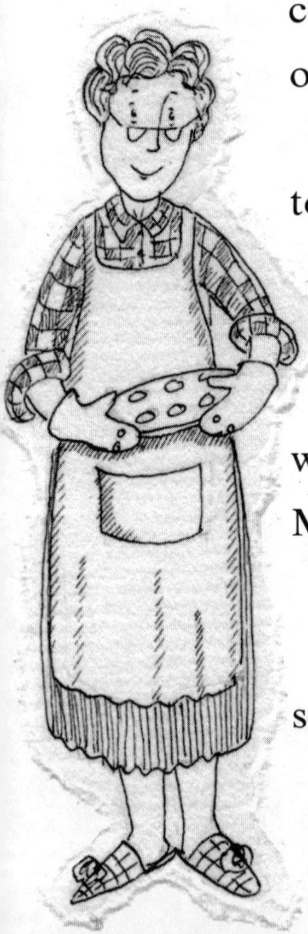

I said, yes, with no tomatoes, mushrooms or cheese.

Granny said she and I would have Pizza and she would do Fish Fingers for Mopsy.

I said to Granny, do sandwiches go blue always?

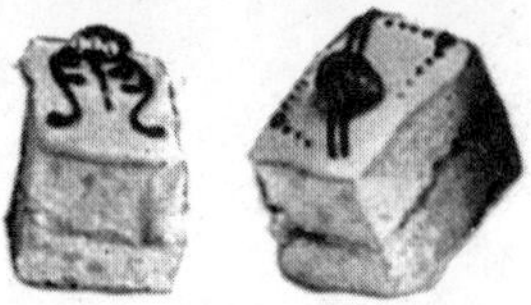

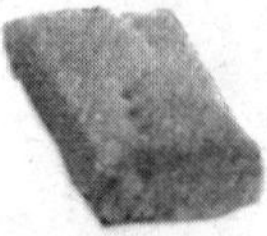

She said, what a funny question. Yes, I suppose so in the end.

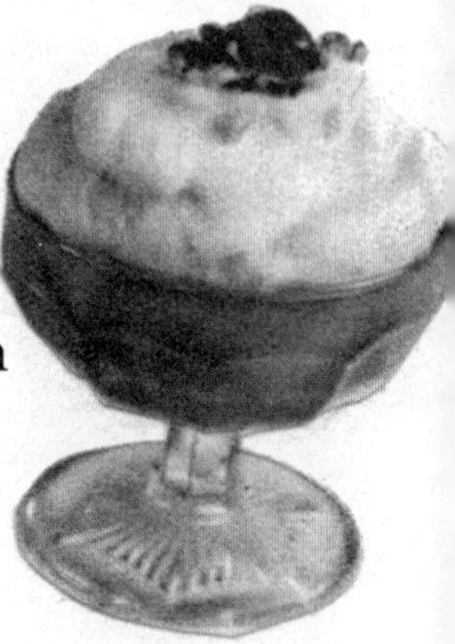

I said, do biscuits go blue?

She said, I've never seen a blue biscuit, come to think of it.

I shall have to save biscuits. I don't like biscuits very much unless they've got chocolate and all our biscuits haven't got chocolate in.

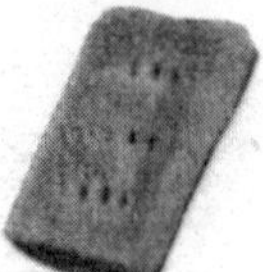

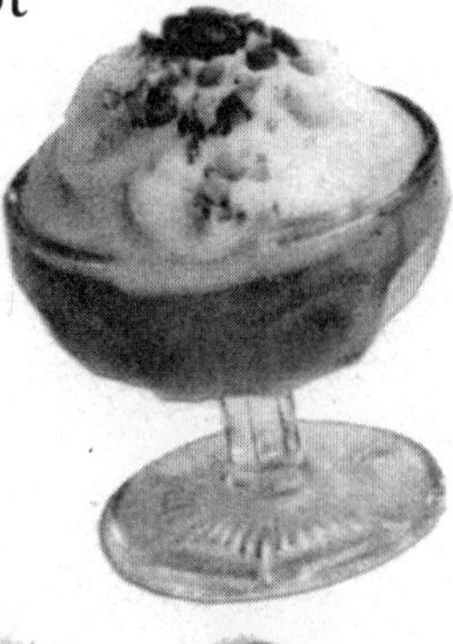

Chocolate Chip Cookies!!! Yum yum bubble gum. Cookies is

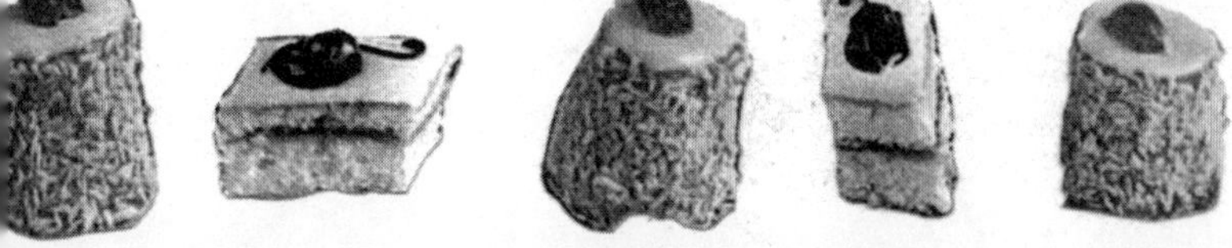

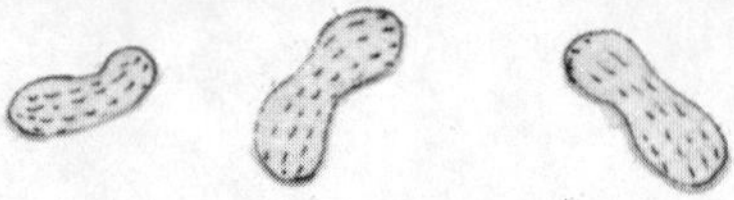

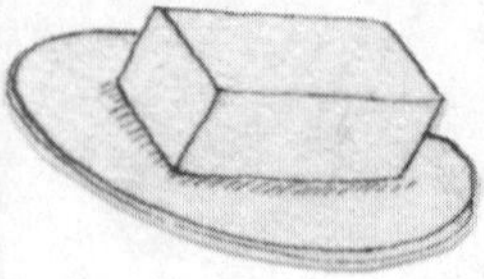

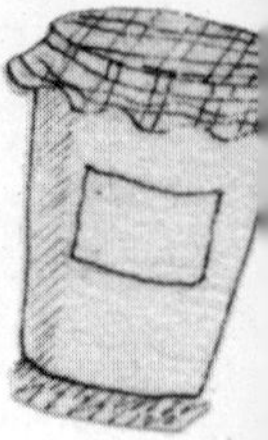

American for biscuits. Americans eat peanut butter and jelly sandwiches, only it's actually jam. They sound disgusting.

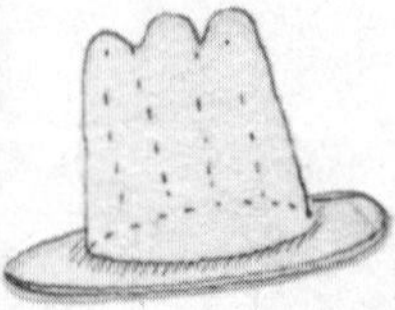

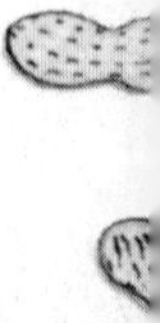

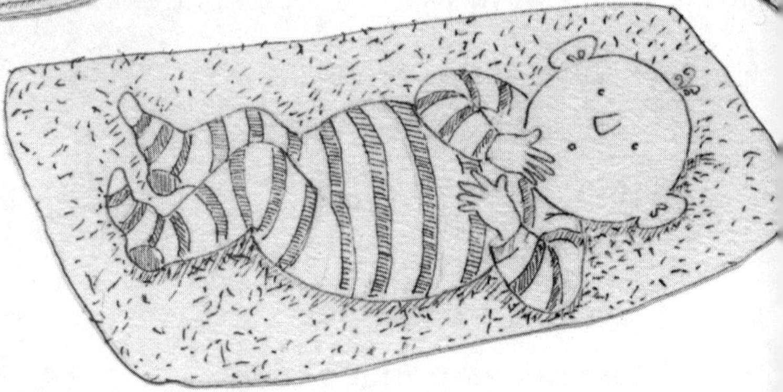

Friday

Mum is coming home tomorrow with It.

I wrote about the new baby in school. Miss Price made everybody clap. This was silly as they don't know what it is like having a new baby.

Darren said his mum had a new baby and it sicked up everywhere.

Granny made peanut butter and jelly meaning jam sandwiches. They were really yummy! Granny tried one too and said they were yummy. She said she had never ever ever had them before in her life and if it hadn't been for me she would never have tried them.

Mopsy wouldn't eat them because of the lumpy bits.

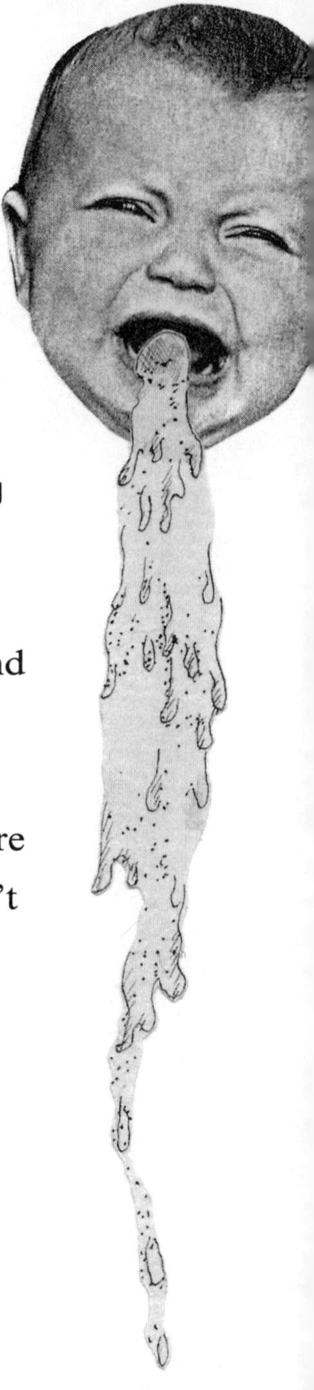

I am sure it is Horace behind the bath.

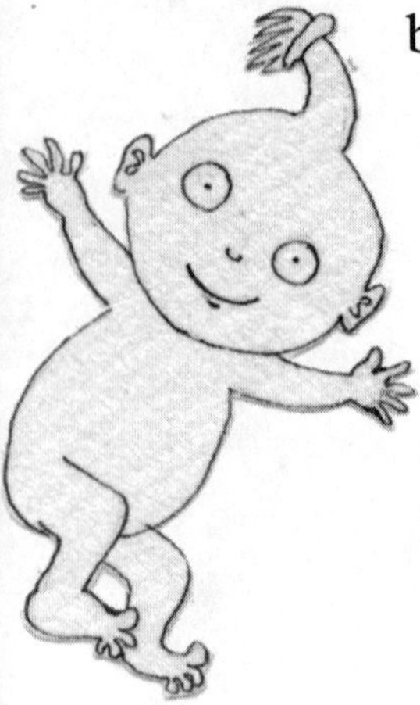

Granny gave me £2!!!

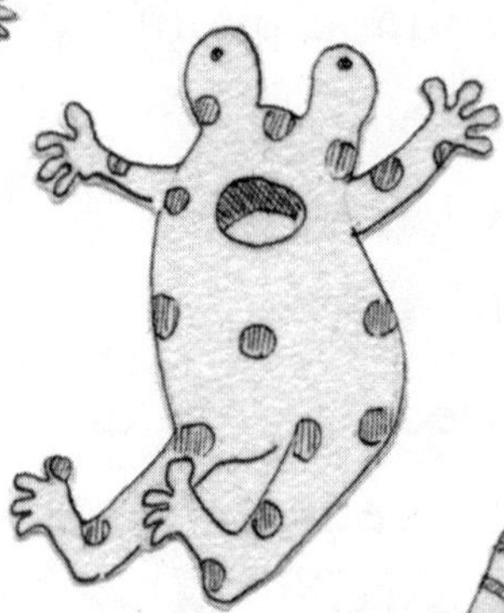

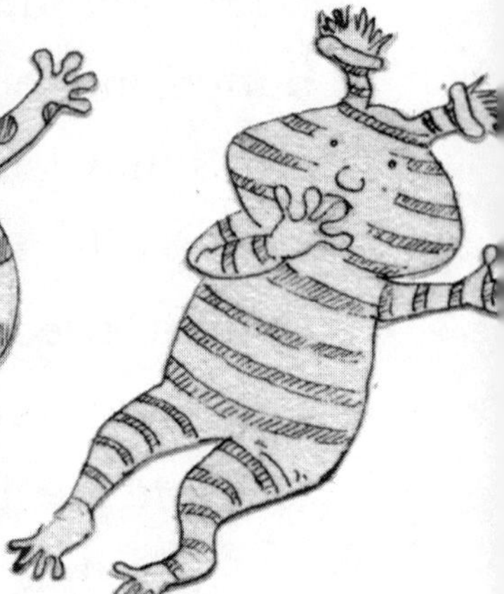

Saturday

It's here. It doesn't look anything like a baby. It is very small and has a red face. I said Mum should take it back and get a proper baby.

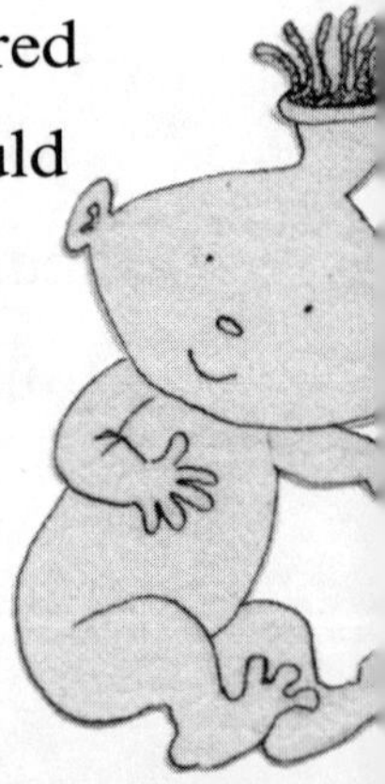

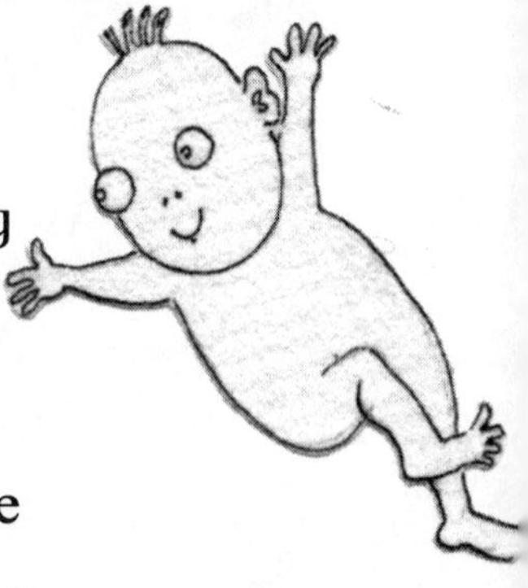

Mopsy is being really silly. She is crying and sucking her thumb. Granny says there there and cuddles her. Granny says she is a bit jealous of the new baby.

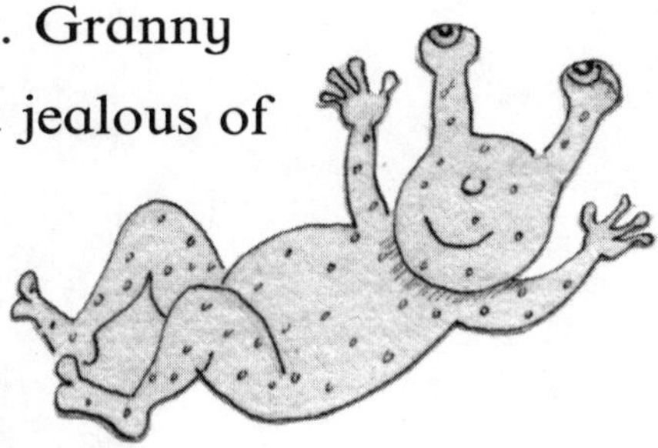

Why?

Dad said, we can't decide what to call him. Have you two got any ideas?

Mopsy said, Tinky Winky.

I said, you can't call him Tinky Winky, stupid.

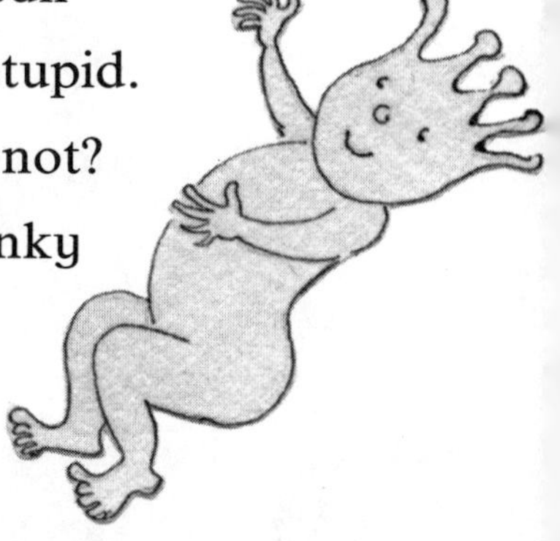

Mopsy said, why not?

I said, because Tinky

Winky isn't a proper name.

She said, yes it is, it's Tinky Winky's proper name.

Dad said, have you got any better suggestions?

I said—I just thought of it—what about William, like William Shakespeare because he ran away from home and became famous.

I didn't mean to say about running away from home. It just came out.

Mum said, mmm William. I like that.

Dad said, it has a good ring to it.

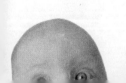

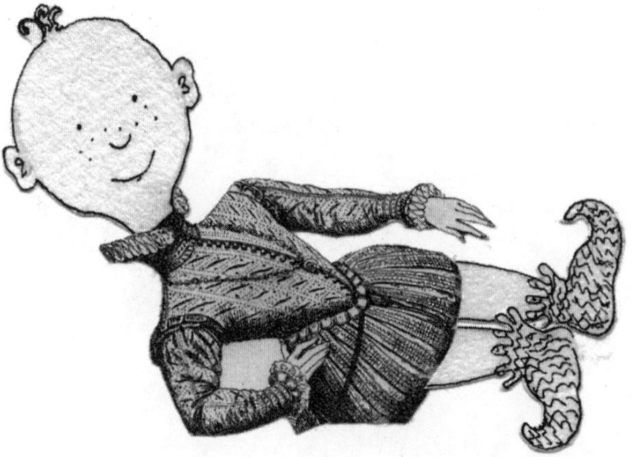

She said, do you look like a William, my poppet?

I said of course he doesn't look like a William, he looks like a tomato. Mum said, shall we call you William, my little tomato?

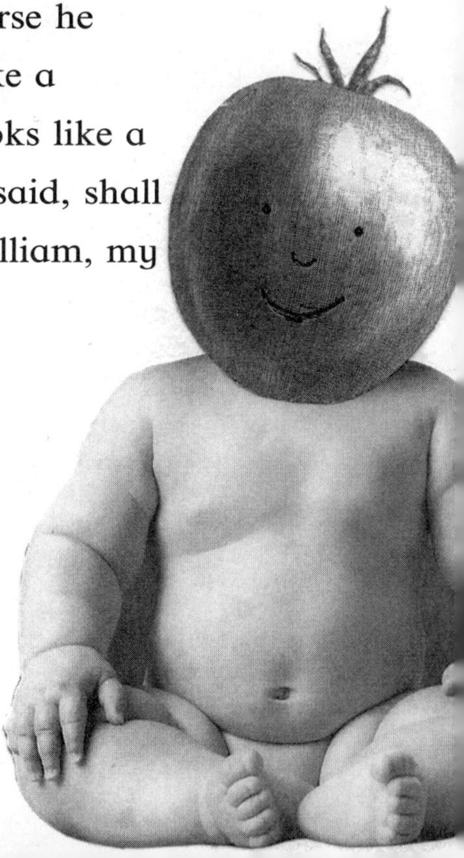

She goes like that when she's talking to him.

Maybe William Shakespeare looked like a tomato once.

It is really gross when she feeds him. I said, Well I never did that. She said, oh yes you did, my darling.

She is lying. I never did that.

Running Away Fund—£3.26!

2 Double Deckers

1 packet salt and vinegar crisps

2 Homemade cakes

2 biscuits

I will give the Snickers bar to Kelly as I really do not like nuts.

Monday

Kelly is being stupid. She says she has another secret only she can't tell me yet and this time it's a really good secret and I will like it.

I DON'T CARE ABOUT HER SECRET. IT IS DUMB.

William has these tiny little hands. The nails look

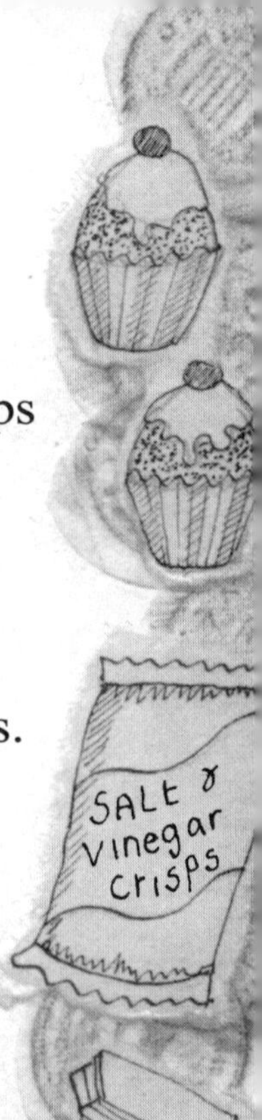
SALT &
vinegar
crisps

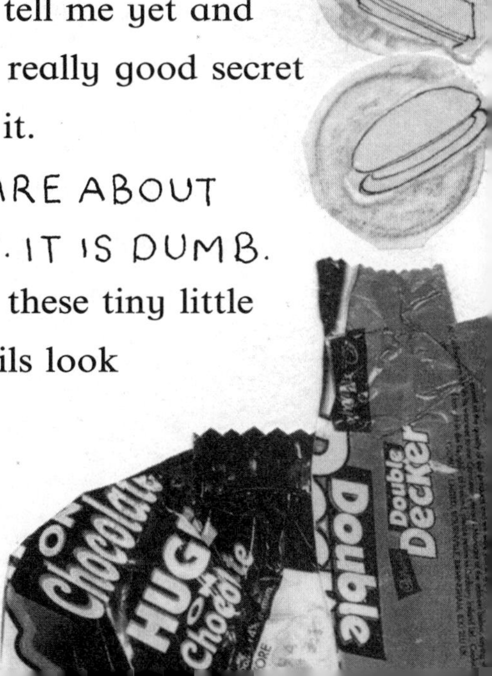
Chocolate
HUGE
Double
Double Decker

frilly. Mum said, put your finger in his hand, and I did and he held it all tightly! Mum says, he knows you're his big sister.

I don't think he does yet.

Mum said it was very nice for him to have a big sister. She was very glad I was his sister. She said I deserved a present for being a nice sister.

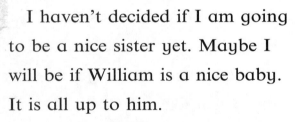

I haven't decided if I am going to be a nice sister yet. Maybe I will be if William is a nice baby. It is all up to him.

Granny is going to make my lunch for the school trip. She said, what do you like and I said, I don't mind.

She said, I'm glad to hear it

because your mummy was an awful fusspot when it came to packed lunches and everything else. I said, did she like brocerly, and Granny said, no, probably not. She hated everything green. She hated peas and salad and beans and carrots. Carrots aren't green but she hated them too.

I said, did she hate lumpy bits? Granny said, I expect so. She wouldn't eat her packed lunch one day because Granny had put special chicken bits in and Mum wouldn't eat it because nobody else had chicken bits and she wanted cheese sandwiches.

I said I'd eat chicken bits, and Granny said, good, but she

didn't actually have any so would peanut butter and jam do and I said yummy.

Tuesday

Today we went to the Tower of London. Darren and Luke were messing about in the bus and Miss Price had to tell them to shut up.

Our Beefeater was called Kevin. They are called Beefeaters because they used to eat lots of beef but they don't have to anymore. They are really called The Yeomen of the Guard. Kevin was quite

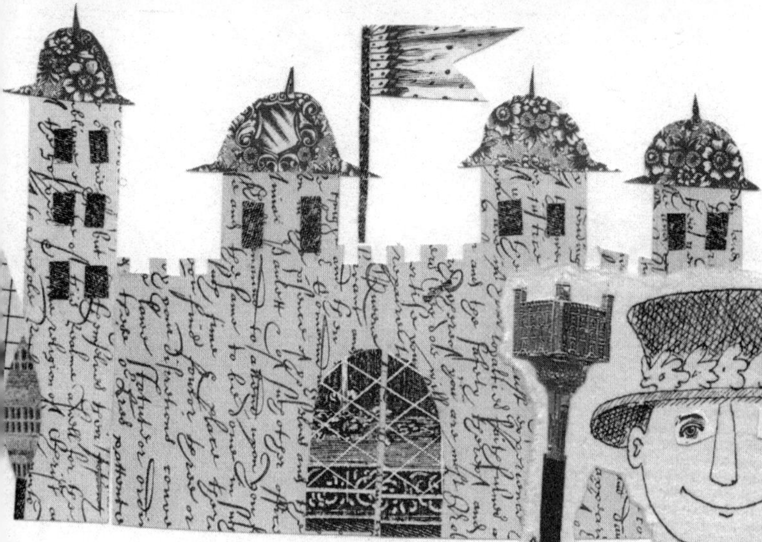

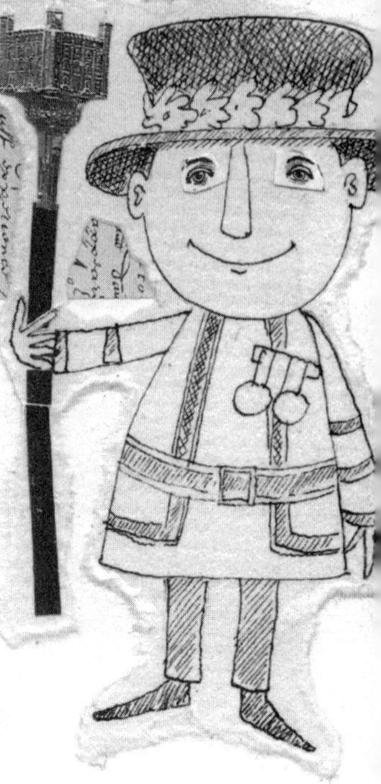

nice but he told all these horrible stories about how people had their heads chopped off. Everybody could have their heads chopped off in those days if they upset Queen Elizabeth. They came up the river and through a gate called Traitor's Gate. There was a tower called The Bloody Tower.

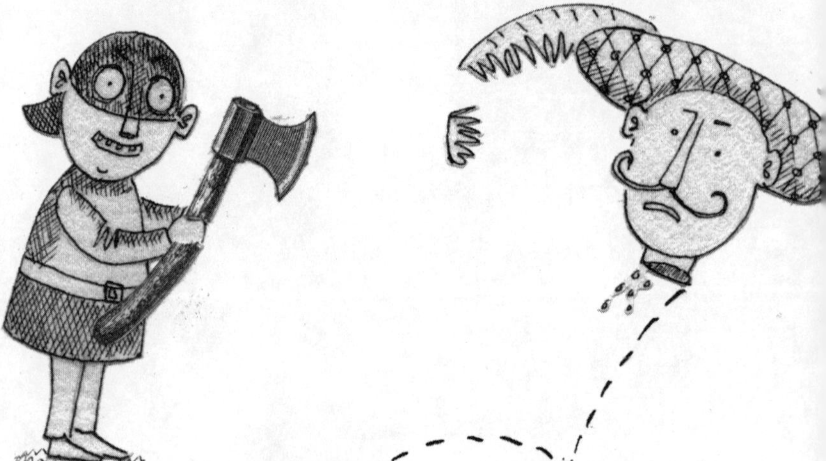

Sometimes it took lots of goes to cut someone's head off as the axe wasn't very sharp. People used to stand around and watch.

All the boys thought it was very funny, but I didn't.

Anyway, I think Kevin was making the stories horrible just for the boys.

Alex pretended to cry

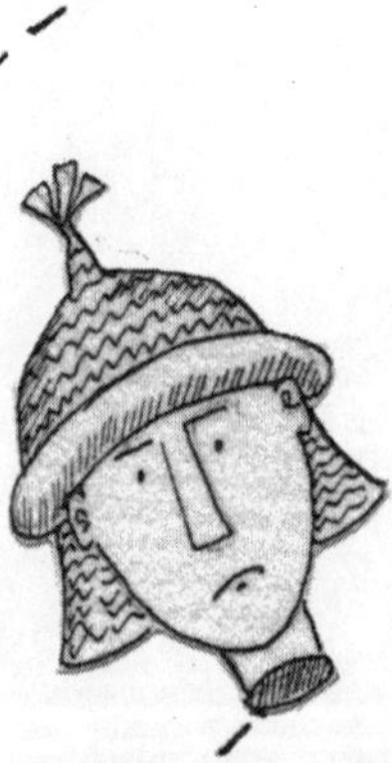

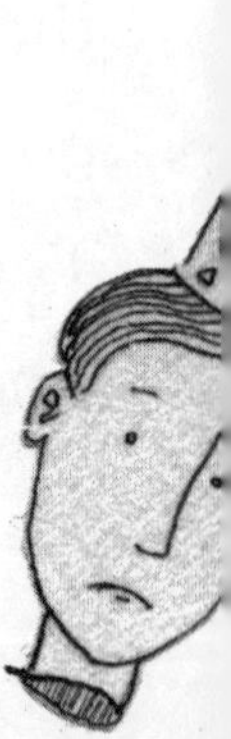

when we saw the place
where they had their heads
chopped off. So of course
we all had to notice her.

The ravens are huge! If
they run away the Tower
will fall down. It is just as
well that it is ravens and
not hamsters.

We saw armor which
was boring and the crown
jewels. We had to wait in
a long long line and then
we had to go by very fast.

They were nice but they would be very heavy to wear. Darren said he would steal the big diamond and I said they would chop his head off if he did. He said he would get his dad to fix them. I said, don't be silly.

Of course, Darren and Luke were nearly late for the bus going back and Miss Price was cross. Then on the way back he kept pretending to chop everyone's heads off with his lunch box. Miss Price said, that's enough Darren and he tried to

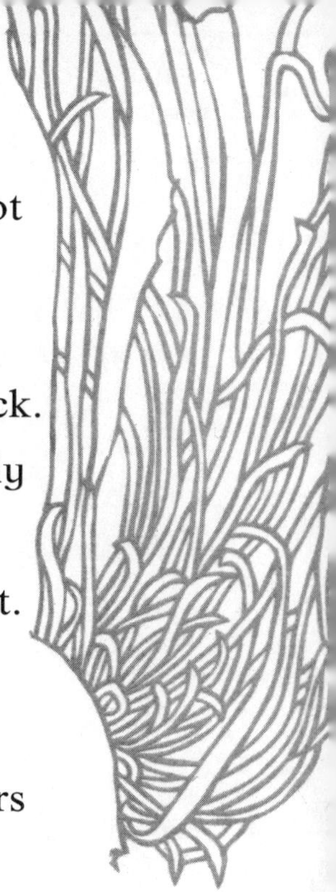

chop her head off. She got really mad then.

Kelly and I sat next to each other on the bus back. She said Lisa wasn't really her sister. But she still wouldn't tell me the secret.

Wednesday

When we finish the Tudors we will do the Greeks.

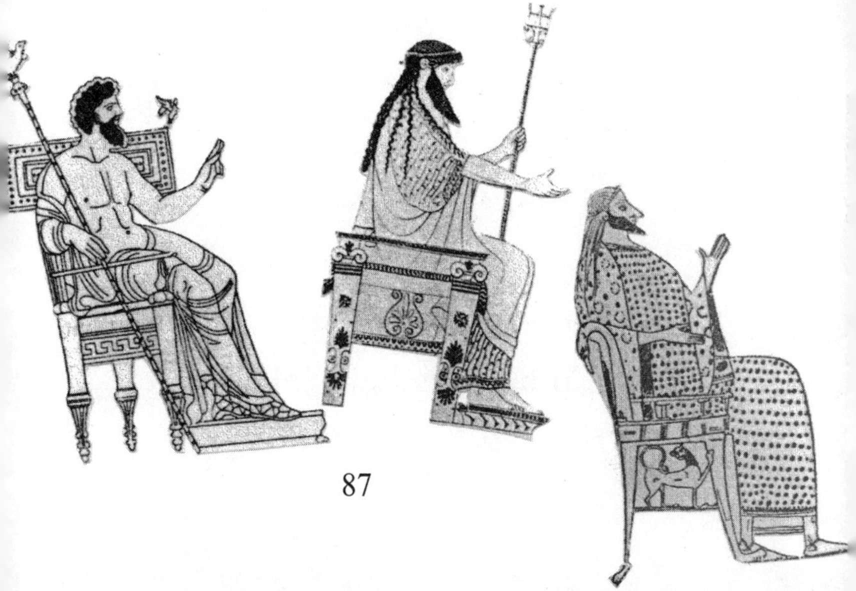

We have twenty spelling
words to learn by Friday!!!
I can do most of them but
not all of them.

Soldier

England

Pretty

Could is easy—I could
spell that when I was one,
I bet.

We are on the eight
times table. That is a
really hard one.

There are painters in the
school and everything
stinks. Mrs. Muldoon says
we have to be very careful
not to bump into them. I
think it is their job to be

$1 \times 8 = 8$

$2 \times 8 = 16$

~~2×8~~

$3 \times 8 = 24$

$4 \times 8 = 32$

$5 \times 8 = 40$

$6 \times 8 = 48$

$7 \times 8 = 56$

$8 \times 8 = 64$

$9 \times 9 = ?$

$10 \times 8 = 80$

$11 \times 8 = 88$

$12 \times 8 = 96$

very careful, not ours.

Darren says all babies do that thing with holding your hand.

Kelly is still going on and on.

I am sure Horace is behind the bath.

We found Horace!

Dad came up and I told him about the noises. He got his screwdriver thing and took a bit of the bath off. Horace was there kind of all scrunched up. Dad

said there was a damp bit
so he had water. He looks
a bit scruffy. We put him
in his cage and gave him
water and food. He just
sat there. I don't think he
was at all grateful.

Hamsters are a bit
boring. A cat would be
nicer.

Alex dresses her cat up and puts him in a baby carriage. She says he likes it. If I was a cat I would not like being put in a carriage by Alex. If we had a cat I would treat it better.

Horace is cute, though. I'm glad he's back.

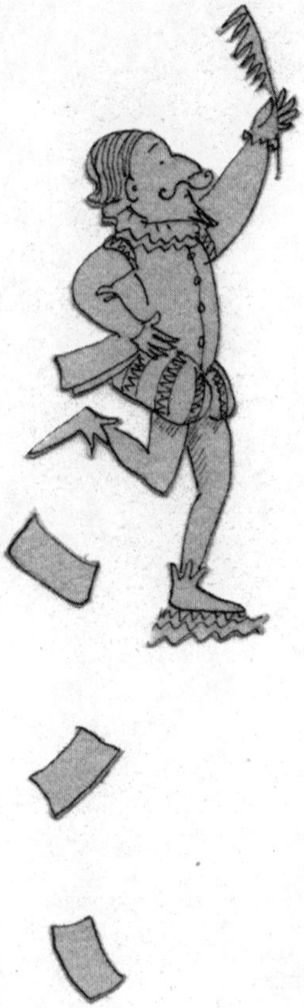

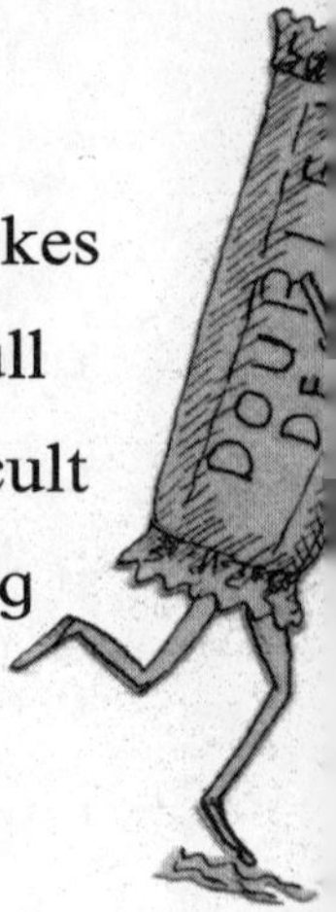

I had to throw the cakes away. They had gone all horrible. It is very difficult to keep food for running away. I wonder what Shakespeare did. They didn't have Double Deckers in his day so it must have been hard.

Thursday

Kelly said, have they told you yet and I said, told me what, and she said, never mind.

I think one of the painters fancies Miss Price. He is the good-looking one. The others are ugly.

He winks at her and says Hallo, Miss when she goes past. She looks all huffy.

But I bet he is better-looking than Nigel. She might as well let him be her boyfriend. I shall tell her this tomorrow.

The phone just rang. Mum took it in the hall and then came and beckoned to Dad and he went out and they were talking. When they came in, they were all giggly. I think they have a secret.

All these secrets are very irritating.

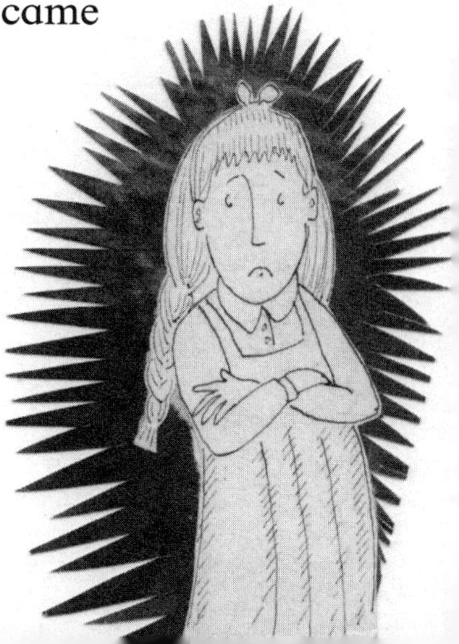

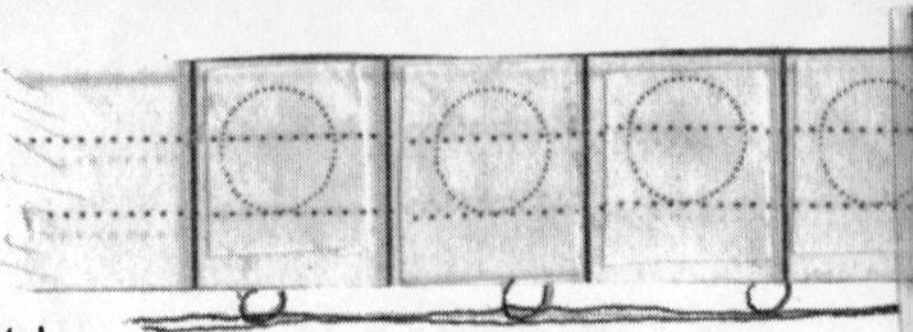

Friday

I KNOW WHAT THE SECRET IS!

It was Kelly's mum on the phone! They want to take me to Disneyland with them!

Mum and Dad said they were talking about it, and I can go!

It is quite soon. We will go on the train and stay in a special hotel. Granny will help them out and give me some money to spend. I told them I already have £3.26 saved, though I did not say what for.

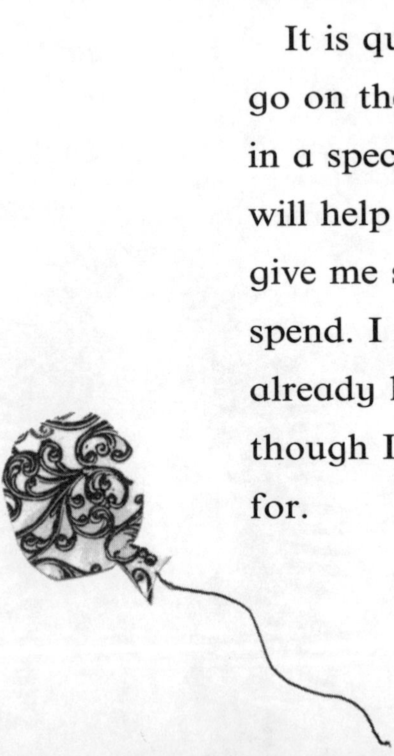

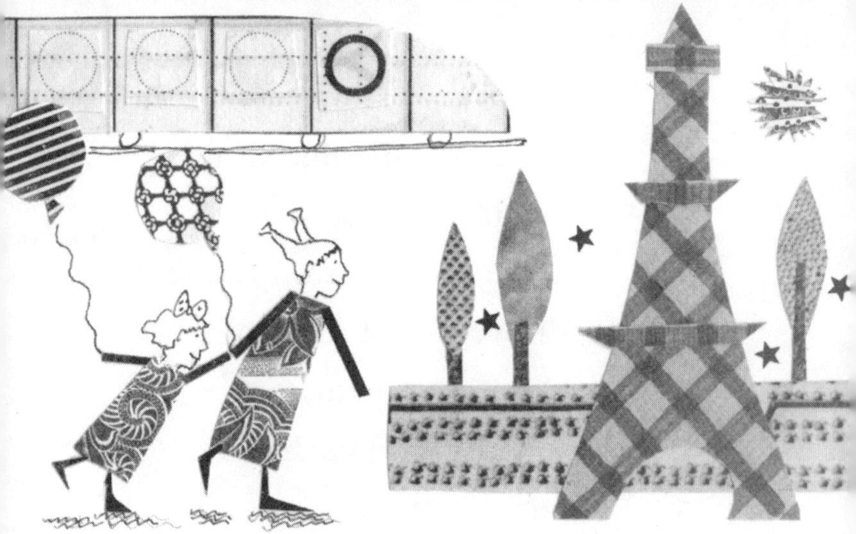

Kelly said she was not allowed to tell me until they had told Mum and Dad.

I told her about pomfreet and I told her about glas. She was very glad I did. We will have lots of pomfreet and glas when we are in France. Kelly is much nicer now. It will be great.

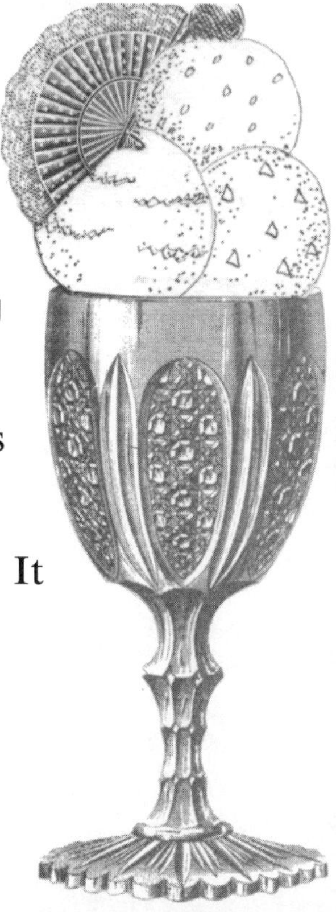

I won't be able to run away for a bit, though I am still going to. Probably I'll wait till I'm grown up like Shakespeare.

Maybe when I come back from Disneyland, William will look like a real baby.

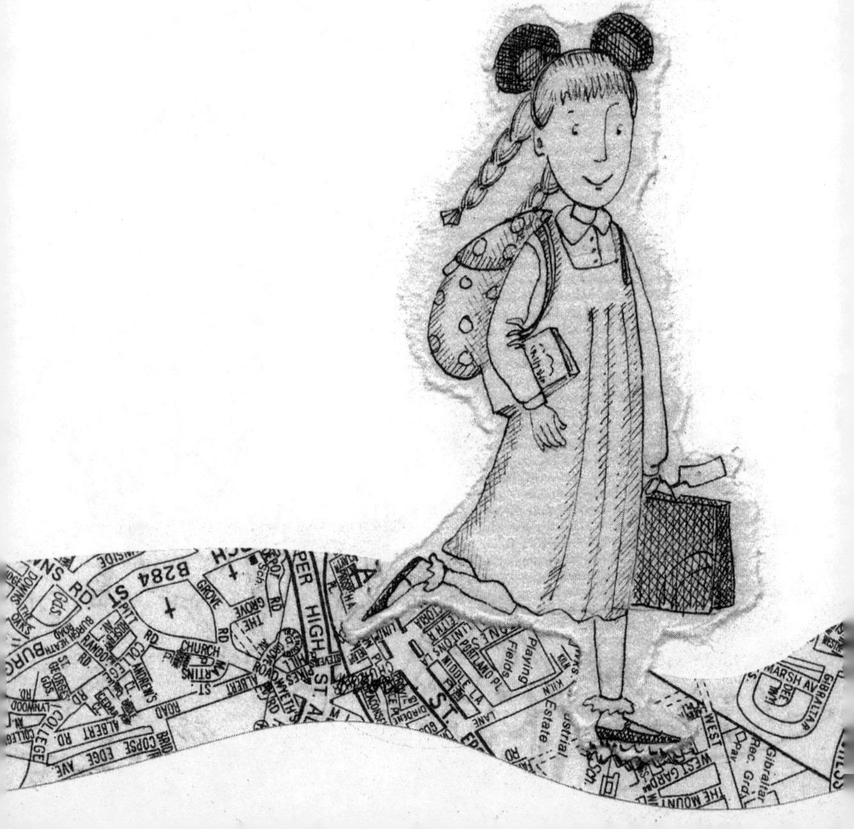
B284
ST
CHURCH
ALBERT RD.
COPSE EDGE AVE
Playing Fields
MIDDLE LA
MARSH AV
Estate
THE MOUNT